THE TIME-TRAVELLING CAT
and the
VIKING TERROR

Other titles by Julia Jarman

THE TIME-TRAVELLING CAT
and the
VIKING TERROR

JULIA JARMAN

Andersen Press • London

First published in 2008 by
Andersen Press Limited,
20 Vauxhall Bridge Road, London SW1V 2SA

Reprinted 2008, 2011

British Library Cataloguing in Publication Data available
ISBN 978 184 270 686 2

Typeset by FiSH Books, Enfield, Middx.
Printed in the UK by CPI Bookmarque, Croydon, CR0 4TD

548 791 4

To Vimla,
an excellent librarian,
and all the Randhawa family,
with thanks for your help and advice.

Acknowledgements

Thanks to friend and author, Theresa Breslin, for a good idea; friend and film maker, Julie Laslett, for her seeing eye; Richard Hall of Jorvik for inspiring lectures about the Vikings; the people at West Stow Anglo-Saxon village for showing me how Anglo-Saxons lived; the Randhawa family for putting me right about Sikh culture; and my new editor, Liz Maude, for asking the right questions.

TOPHER'S JOURNEY
✖✖✖ A.D. 868 ✖✖✖

THE
WASH

EAST ANGLIA

River Ouse

NORWICH

HAEGELLISDOM

River Yare

NORFOLK

SWINDUNE
ELY

THETFORD

River Waveney

BURY (St Edmunds)

SUFFOLK

N
W   E
S

┼┼┼┼ CAUSEWAY
- - - - TOPHER'S ROUTE

Chapter 1

'Ka's missing, and I don't want to come.'

Topher was on the phone to Ellie, one of his best friends. She was in North London where he used to live. He lived near Chichester now, in a house with a big garden that Ka loved. Sitting on the kitchen table, he scanned the sloping lawn, hoping to see her emerge from under one of the trees.

'She will come back, Topher. She always does.' Ellie sounded exasperated, and he pictured her raking her fingers through her dark hair. He'd been planning to spend the beginning of the summer break with her. They always got together in the holidays.

'I know. But—'

He wondered how to explain why he was so worried. How could he say that he thought Ka was time-travelling? Ellie was very understanding about most things, but when he'd tried to tell her – after Ka's first journey to Ancient Egypt – she'd laughed. When he'd persisted she'd looked at him as if he were crazy. So he hadn't told her, or that he had been too. Ellie knew that he worried about Ka, but not why – that she was often in terrible danger. People in the past were often cruel. Ellie just thought that Ka was one of those cats who had several homes, which she had in a way.

'And when she comes back,' Ellie went on, 'Molly will look after her. She's good with animals.'

Molly was Topher's stepmum and Ellie was right about her. Molly had a cat of her own called Buggins. Topher could see him now, a big fat tabby, fast asleep in his box by the central heating boiler, even though it was a warm day.

'I'd still rather wait,' he said stubbornly, still scanning the garden. Ka's favourite hiding place was a willow tree near the pond.

'I know what it is.' Ellie gave one of her annoying knowing laughs. 'It's not about Ka at all. You're scared of terrorists.'

'I'm not.' Well, he hadn't been till she mentioned it. Now though, he remembered hearing warnings. There had been a spate of terrorist attacks in London and security experts said there were bound to be more. Perhaps it would be better to stay here? Or Ellie could come and stay with him?

'Topher, listen to me.' Ellie was very bossy sometimes. 'If we let these suicide bombers stop us doing what we want to do, we're letting them win. We're letting them change our way of life.'

'Yes, yes.' He knew all that. 'I'd still rather wait till Ka comes back, okay? Then bring her with me so she can visit all her old haunts.'

Ka had first turned up when he lived in London, soon after his mum had died. She'd helped him get over that terrible time.

'Topher, you can't let your life be ruled by a cat.'

'Ka is not just any cat, Ellie.'

*

2

Luckily the doorbell rang, so he went to open it, walking from the kitchen through the oak-lined hallway, with Ellie still jabbering in his ear. Before opening the door, he peered through the diamond-paned window at the side.

'Topher, is that Sanjit?'

Sanjit Daas was a mate from school – and as Ellie pointed out – he was another reason for sticking to what they'd planned. Sanjit was going to London too, to stay with his auntie, who also lived in Archway. His parents were taking them. Topher's would fetch them back. It was all arranged.

'Topher, let me talk to Sanjit.' Ellie never gave up.

Jabber. Jabber. Jabber.

'That's settled then,' she said when he got the phone back. 'You're both coming and we'll do exactly what we planned to do, while keeping a lookout for suspicious goings-on.'

Sanjit grinned. 'Just agree with her, mate. It's easier. If anyone should be worried it's me. You'll be okay, with your Viking looks. With my dusky features I'll be a suspicious going-on. My cousins are having a terrible time, being stopped by the police every five minutes. '

'With your face you'll be chased all round London by girls going, "Ooh! Aah! Look at his gorgeous eyelashes!"'

'And if they do my bibi will bash them with her chapatti pan!'

Sanjit's bibi, his grandma, lived with his auntie. She came from the Punjab and had very old-fashioned ideas, unlike Sanjit who was into all the latest gear.

He shouted into the phone, ''Bye, Ellie!' and headed upstairs to Topher's bedroom. 'Let's see this latest game of yours, mate. I hope it's more up to date than your chinos.'

They spent the rest of the afternoon playing on Topher's Xbox and Sanjit won most of the games.

They stayed in Topher's room and he found it hard to concentrate. It was a big room overlooking the front garden, and his computer and all his books and lots of other stuff were there. But it was the statue of Ka beside his bed, which kept distracting him. He couldn't help turning round to look at it, because it was proof that Ka was time-travelling. When she was a real live cat in the present day it wasn't there. When she went time-travelling it was. It was as if she left a replica of herself behind, so he wouldn't forget what she looked like. As if he could. After a bit Sanjit noticed him looking at it and went to look more closely himself. He'd never seen it before and spotted the likeness immediately.

'It's amazing. Did the sculptor model it from life?'

'Dunno. My mum brought it back from Egypt.' She'd said it was old, but he didn't tell Sanjit that.

'Is that your mum?' He'd spotted the photo beside the cat. 'She looks like you. Did she show the sculptor a photograph?'

'No. She couldn't have. Ka turned up after she died.'

That was true, but not as straightforward as it sounded. Sometimes he felt sure his mum had met Ka

4

before, but it was a mystery. Time was complicated, but he didn't say that either.

Sanjit picked up the statue and weighed it in his hand. 'What's it made of?'

'Sardonyx, a sort of stone.'

It was reddish gold with black and white specks – like Ka. Exactly like a seated Ka, right down to the shiny black key-like mark on her forehead, the holy ankh, the Egyptian sign of life. Except that Ka was flesh and blood and fur. Longing to stroke her fur again, he took the statue from Sanjit. How heavy and cold and dull it was. That meant Ka was a long way away – in space and time. When she was returning the stone became warm and shone. If only it would happen again soon. But it wouldn't, not while Sanjit was here.

While he was putting it back beside his bed his mobile rang. Ellie again. He flopped down on his red beanbag.

'Topher, I've been thinking.'

'Wow!'

'Stop it! I've been thinking about terrorists. Actually I've just read this article. It says you're more likely to die of smoking ...'

'I don't smoke.'

'Shut up ... even passive smoking, or being run over, than you are of being killed by a terrorist.'

'So?'

'It's a minute, an *infinitesimal* risk.' Ellie liked big words.

'Ellie, I am not scared of terrorists even though experts

have said a terrorist attack is probable even inevitable.'
He could use big words too. 'I'm worried about Ka.'

He was lying again. He *was* a bit scared when he
thought about it. Who wasn't? Terrorists terrorised just
by threatening to attack. And he had a funny feeling –
funny-weird not funny-ha ha – that something bad was
going to happen. He always did when Ka was away.

Ellie said, 'Ka will be all right. Remember, she's got
nine lives.'

That was probably true.

'But I've only got one,' he said, though that wasn't.

Sanjit stayed on for another game and then a meal.
Longing to be alone in his bedroom, Topher wasn't too
pleased when Molly came home and invited Sanjit to
stay to supper. It was another hour before his dad got
home from work – with Tally, Topher's baby sister, who
he'd picked up from nursery. Then they ate outside, on
the terrace overlooking the garden.

'Poulet basquaise!' said Molly plonking a heavy dish
on the table.

'Chicken in t-tomato sauce,' translated Chris Hope,
struggling to put Tally into her baby seat.

Topher and his dad shared the same name –
Christopher Hope. It had been Topher's mum's idea to
call one of them Chris, the other Topher, to avoid
confusion.

'And roast potatoes,' Molly said, putting another dish
on the table. 'Specially for you, Topher. And I've done
some sauce without chicken for you too. You can have

cheese on it. Where's Ka, by the way? She usually appears at meal times.'

Topher, who was vegetarian, had been thinking the same thing. The aroma of spicy tomato sauce reminded him of their trip to the Aztecs. He hoped she hadn't gone back there. That had been one of their scariest adventures.

Sanjit said, 'Mr Hope, I have seen the statue of Ka in Topher's bedroom. It is amazingly like her.'

'Yes, and probably very valuable. Topher's mum brought it back from Egypt. It's an antique, but some-times – you won't believe this – he loses it. It simply disappears and he has no idea where it is.'

'He doesn't really lose it,' said Molly. 'It's just that his bedroom is so untidy, he can't find it sometimes. No, Tally!'

The baby was grabbing Molly's long black hair. Topher loved his stepmum. She was much more understanding than his dad, who was older than her. Old and bald and grumpy, he wore glasses that made him look like an absent-minded professor. Not that Molly seemed to mind. She seemed to think he was great. They were both scientists and very clever, but neither of them had a clue about the link between the statue and Ka.

Later, after Sanjit had gone home, Topher went to bed quite early so he could watch the statue. It was on his bedside cabinet, exactly where he'd left it, next to a photo of his mum. Evening sunlight shone through the diamond-shaped windowpanes, making her long fair hair, the same colour as his, glow like gold, but the statue looked dull. Wishing it were winter so darkness would come quickly, he got into bed. Then lying on his side facing the statue, he murmured, 'Ka, come back to me. Come back to me.'

Gradually it got darker, but nothing happened. It looked dull and it felt cold. But when he woke in the middle of the night, it was shining.

Chapter 2

It was happening.

The statue's eyes gleamed, and on the wall opposite circles of light moved from left to right and back again. Left right, back again. Left right, back again. And he had to force himself to stop looking at the mesmerising pattern and turn to look at the statue. At Ka, for it was clearly her, though for the moment, only her head was covered with fur, short fur like velvet. Her large triangular ears were golden, the ankh on her forehead black and glossy, but the rest of her body was still molten stone rippling and flickering as if someone or something was breathing life into it.

'Mwa!' She opened her mouth, revealing a diamond of pink, outlined with tiny white teeth.

'Mwa!' She cried again, louder, making him wonder if she was hurting, and he saw her pink tongue flick as white whiskers sprang from either side of her mouth.

And now the furriness was spreading in all directions. Rapidly. As he watched, fur grew from her sticking out shoulder blades, then her front legs, and suddenly white claws like tiny cutlasses sprang one by one from her golden paws.

'Mwa-a!' It was a gasp. 'T-touch me, Topher!'

He reached out and scratched between her ears. She loved that. Then he stroked under her furry chin, longing to feel purrs throbbing against his fingers.

'You're okay. You're home now.'

But she wasn't yet completely home. More slowly now, hair by hair, tuft by tuft, golden fur flecked with black and white grew out of her back, then her hind legs became furry, and last of all, her long tail fluffed up like a bottle-brush, before settling and becoming sleek as she curled it round her body. A real cat again, she began to purr. Prrr. Prrrrr. Like a small tractor, but not for long.

'Mwow!'

Suddenly she sprang to the floor and headed for the door.

'You're hungry?'

Grabbing the torch he kept by his bed, he crept after her as she led the way onto the landing. He didn't want to wake anyone, least of all Tally, who would bawl for hours in the middle of the night if she woke up and no one would play with her. So he suppressed a laugh at the sight of Ka's bum bobbing down the stairs in front of him. At the base of her upright tail, it looked just like the full stop at the bottom of an exclamation mark.

'Where have you been, Ka?' He risked a whisper when they were in the kitchen and he was filling her dish with Whiskas. But she didn't answer, though she could speak and sometimes did. He'd switched on the copper light that hung over the big oak table. He wanted to examine her in case she'd been injured. She had been when she'd travelled to Tudor times, but when he tried to part her fur with his fingers she turned and nipped his hand. It was cat-language for 'Go away, I want to eat in peace'. So he went to the fridge and cut her a few cubes of cheese. Cheese was her favourite treat, and he thought she might like some for pudding, but when she'd finished the Whiskas, she headed back upstairs. Again he followed her – with the cheese for morning – and he reached his bedroom as she disappeared under the duvet, her favourite sleeping place.

It was lovely to curl his body round her – she was like a hot water bottle – and bliss to feel her there when he woke up, and to realise it was Saturday. Waking her gently, he gave her some cheese, then went to his desk and switched on his computer. Then he lifted her onto his knee and said, 'Where did you go, Ka?' – because she sometimes replied by typing on his computer. But she wasn't in the mood for writing, and when he offered her more cheese she jumped off his knee. Hearing birds outside she sprang onto the windowsill.

'Miaow!' She wanted to go out.

'Well, come back soon.' He opened the window and she jumped down onto the conservatory roof. Seconds later he saw her in the garden, on the lawn, heading for the neighbour's tidy vegetable patch.

Soon afterwards he heard Tally yelling for Molly and the day began. When he saw Ka again they were all in the kitchen eating breakfast. She came in through the cat flap, but it was mid-morning before he got a chance to question her in the privacy of his bedroom. She came and sat on his knee while he was playing a computer game.

'Where did you go, Ka?'

Again she kept him waiting, circling and kneading his chinos with her claws. It was as if she was thinking, or even teasing. As he waited, trying not to show his impatience, he nuzzled her fur, which smelled of the wheat fields behind their house.

'Don't tell me you've only been chasing mice in the back field.'

She gave him a sidelong glance, then put out a paw and pressed the keyboard, as Tally toddled in, hands outstretched. 'Pussy!'

Ka was out of the room and onto the landing in a flash. She was the gentlest, most tolerant of cats, but she drew the limit at Tally's so-called cuddles. Quickly Topher pressed SAVE as Tally set off in pursuit of Ka.

'No, you don't.' He caught his little sister at the top of the stairs, trying to open the stair-gate.

When he returned to his room the computer screen was dark. He pressed the mouse and a word appeared, well a sort of word.

HaEgeLL;;;;

He sat down to study it closely. What did it mean? He longed to ask Ka to explain, but when would he get a chance? It was a Saturday so the rest of the family was at home all day, unless they went shopping. Now that Tally was walking, Ka tended to stay outside till evening. He searched the garden calling her name, but she didn't appear, and the day seemed to drag. Haegel. Heggel. Haggle. HELL. Strange words kept coming into his mind.

Chapter 3

It was seven o'clock before Ka returned. Topher had just said goodnight to Tally, when he saw her from the landing window. She was creeping out from under the willow tree at the bottom of the garden. For a few minutes she sat on the grass watching the upstairs windows, then – at the exact moment that Tally's bedroom curtains swished shut – she raced to the kitchen door. Topher rushed down to let her in and fill her dish.

'What's this about going to hell?'

She gave him a disdainful look and went back to eating. Luckily Molly and his dad were still upstairs, so he could talk to her without seeming barmy.

'Are you going to tell me where you went?'

She didn't answer, but when Molly did come into the kitchen, she left her dish and led the way to his bedroom.

The computer was still on and she jumped onto the chair in front of it. But then she began to wash.

'You're a rotten tease.'

She washed herself thoroughly, as if determined to lick every hair on her body, even in the hard to reach place between her shoulder blades. He couldn't help admiring the way she did that, twisting her head round and stretching her rough pink tongue.

'Finished now?'

No. Using her right front paw as a flannel she started to wash her face, right side first, pulling her ear forward, to wash behind it, then letting it flick back.

'At last!'

But she washed the other side, before turning to the screen where he'd put up what she'd written before.

HaEgeLL

'What does that mean?'

She licked her right paw again.

'It's spotless!'

She gave it one more lick then held it out over the top row of letters, as if she were thinking which letter to press. Then she pressed more letters.

HaEgeLLiSDOM

'Haegellisdom?' It sounded as if it could be a place. 'What happened there?'

She gave him a long stare, then jumped onto his bed, circled a few of times and settled down on the blue duvet, with her tail over her eyes. It was her DO NOT DISTURB sign. She must have had a busy day – or perhaps she didn't want to think about what had happened at Haegellisdom. Or perhaps she thought she'd done enough. He could find out what had happened.

He googled up Haegellisdom and found that it was the old name for Hellesdon, a village in Norfolk, not far from Norwich. The word was Anglo-Saxon and meant the hill of a man called Haegel. There was a photo of a sleepy looking modern village, well modern except for a few thatched cottages. Its only claim to fame was that in 870 it had been the scene of a battle between the Anglo-Saxons and the Vikings, who were led by a chief called Ingwar the Boneless.

'Boneless! How did he stand up? ' He turned to Ka, but she was snoring.

With nothing better to do, he googled up Ingwar.

Called both Ingwar the Boneless and Ingwar the Fox – because of his great cunning – he was son of the Viking leader, Ragnar Lothbrok, or Hairy Britches, and his second wife, Aslaug. Angry with Ragnar, because he lay with her before she wished, Aslaug put a curse on their first child before it was born. When she gave birth to a boy, the child had no bones. Where his bones should have been there was only gristle. Never able to walk, he reached a great height – nine feet or 2.70 metres tall some say – and grew up to be a bloodthirsty warrior. He was infamous for devising the gruesome killing, called blood or spread eagling. Angry with Aella, King of the Northumbrians, he ordered his men to saw through the King's ribs and remove them, then rip out his lungs and spread them either side of him to resemble the wings of an eagle.

'Did you see that, Ka?'

But she slept on and he scrolled down to find out more. Topher read that Ingwar couldn't stand up, so he had to be carried everywhere.

Unable to walk unaided, he wore a frame like a cage to stop him flopping all over the place, and his guards carried him everywhere. In battles they held him high, so he could glare down on the enemy, some of whom ran away at the mere sight of him.

'What are you looking at, lad?' Chris Hope came in, most likely to check Topher wasn't in any unsuitable chat rooms. Seeing he wasn't, he took a look round the room. 'The usual tip I see, and your statue's gone undercover again.'

Best to ignore that. 'I'm reading about the Vikings.'

'History.' His dad looked approving. 'Well, that's better than violent computer games.'

'You think so? Look at this.' He pointed to the bit about spread-eagling.

'Ingwar the Boneless.' His dad laughed. 'Sounds like someone in a story to me. Don't believe everything you read on the internet.'

He left the room, but came back soon afterwards with a book.

'Have a look at this. It will be a bit more reliable. Your mum and I got it from the British Museum. We saw that.' He pointed to the cover where there was a photo of a horse's head made of gold. 'Just look at the detail there. There's more inside. The Vikings were very creative, and well organised but you don't hear about that.'

'Well, Ingwar was destructive. He killed loads of people.'

'If he really existed.' His dad pointed to the screen again. 'Doesn't it say there that most info about him comes from the sagas? Oh no.' He stopped to listen. 'That sounds like Tally's crying.'

As his dad went to see what his little sister wanted, Topher scanned the book's index but there was no mention of Ingwar. Later though, on another website, he found a date for the gruesome murder of King Aella. So he must have existed.

> Ingwar was the mastermind behind the attacks on the English mainland in the final quarter of the ninth century. The murder of King Aella of the Northumbrians in 867 was an act of revenge, for Aella had murdered Ingwar's own father, Ragnor Lothbrook. Aella had had Ragnor thrown into a pit of poisonous snakes. As he died, Ragnor cried out, 'How the little pigs would grunt if they knew how it fared with the old boar!' By 'little pigs' he meant his four sons, and when they did hear about it they all vowed to exact bloody revenge. Hvitserk was playing chess when he heard and he gripped the piece so hard that blood spurted from his fingernails. Sigurd, who was cutting his nails at the time, cut straight through to the bone, and Bjorn grabbed a spear so tightly that he left the print of his fingers in it. But Ingwar, the fourth son, showed little emotion. He simply swore that he would avenge his father's death in the time-honoured Viking fashion of blood-eagling.

Time honoured? So he hadn't invented blood-eagling, but it was definitely his speciality. All the experts seemed to agree about that, though they couldn't agree where Haegellisdom was. A dozen places disputed the Norfolk Hellesdon's claim. All they could say for sure was that it was in East Anglia.

'What do you think, Ka?'

17

He leaned over to stroke her. She lowered her tail and looked at him with her round amber eyes.

'This Ingwar...'

But at the sound of the name she stiffened and jumped off the bed.

'Well, don't go there again,' he pleaded as she headed for the door. 'Promise!'

It was worrying. Did she choose whether to time-travel or not? He'd been on four journeys with her now, but he still didn't know.

Chapter 4

Ka made it very clear she didn't want to hear about the Vikings. Whenever he mentioned them she left the room. But she didn't go far. She was usually in another room or the garden and when she saw Topher packing his bag to go to Ellie's, she stayed very close indeed.

'You want to come with me?'

Of cou...rrrse. Of cou...rrrse. She purred like a tractor and rubbed against his legs.

'Good. I want you to come with me.'

He was glad she liked travelling in the car.

On Wednesday morning when the Daas family came to pick Topher up, she bounded into their Renault and settled on Topher's knee in the seat behind the driver. And that was fine – till Mrs Daas turned round to tell Sanjit to do up his seat belt and shrieked.

Amazingly Ka stayed on Topher's knee, gripping with her claws. Topher could hardly believe it. Mrs Daas was usually so calm. He'd never heard her shout before. Come to think of it, he'd never seen her in traditional dress before either. She was wearing a gold and black sari, and Mr Daas was wearing a black turban. When Topher had been round their house before, the Daas had always worn fashionable western clothes, and Mrs Daas had been really friendly. Now she was clambering out of the car.

'Mum.' Sanjit followed her. 'It's all right. It's Ka, Topher's pet cat and she's ever so nice.' Sanjit was dressed as usual in shirt and jeans. So were two of his sisters, Radha and Davina, who were giggling on the back seat. But the eldest, Rekha, wore a pink sari. She said, 'Sanjit's wasting his time. I'm sorry, Topher, but it doesn't make any difference how nice your cat is. Mum can't stand them.'

Sanjit got back in. 'Why on earth didn't you say you wanted to bring Ka, mate? Most people don't bring their cats on trips to London.'

Outside on the pavement, Molly was trying to reassure Mrs Daas.

'Really. It will be okay. Ka likes travelling. She's a very unusual cat, more like a dog in some ways. She'll stay on Topher's knee, you'll see.'

But that was no comfort to Mrs Daas, who didn't like dogs either.

In the end a compromise was reached. Ka could come, but only if she travelled on the back seat, in a cat basket. Molly fetched it from the attic. Topher persuaded her to go in, while everyone changed places in the car. They only set off when Topher and Ka were sitting at the back as far from Mrs Daas as they could get.

Ka hated the basket which she associated with the vets and injections. Topher thought she might yowl all the way, but she was very good and stayed still and silent for most of the journey. It was only when they reached the outskirts of London that she became a bit agitated. Mr Daas had to keep stopping and starting the car, sometimes suddenly, for traffic and traffic lights, and once at a checkpoint. It was on the road to Hammersmith Bridge, as they were about to cross the Thames. The area was swarming with police. As Topher glanced at a backdrop of houses and high-rise flats, Mr Daas switched on the radio, and they found out why. A newsreader was announcing a terrorist alert.

'Oh no,' said Sanjit. 'I can see what my so-called holiday's going to be like. It'll be stop and search every five minutes. Hello hello hello. Have you got a bomb in your pocket, young man?'

His dad told him off. 'Just remember it's for the benefit of all of us. Everyone is being stopped, can't you see? We must all be tolerant and vigilant. You know why.' The car crawled forward and then stopped again. Police were stopping all vehicles and waving most of them on, but some drivers had to pull in, get out of their car and hand over their documents. Topher couldn't help admiring Mr and Mrs Daas' patience. While they waited Mr Daas listened to the cricket and Mrs Daas took the opportunity to feed everyone with samosas and parothas. His dad would have been drumming his fingers on the dashboard by now, and Molly would have been trying to calm him down. When Mr Daas had to pull in and show his driving licence to a policeman, he was very polite. When Topher rang the Wentworths to tell them of the delay, Ellie's mum went into a tirade about civil liberties.

'We're becoming a police state, Topher, we really are! Please give Mr and Mrs Daas my sympathy and say I hope you get here before the rush hour.'

*

21

Eventually they arrived at Cheverton Road, and stopped for a moment in the tree-lined road while Topher tried to remember which of the terraced houses was the Wentworths'. The Victorian houses with their higgledy-piggledy rooftops all looked alike at first glance. Then a bright red door opened and Ellie rushed out to greet them. Her brothers, Luke and Russell, dressed as pirates, rushed out after her, followed by Ellie's mum, who urged them all to come in for a cup of tea. But Mrs Daas declined saying they were all expected at her sister-in-law's house and Sanjit's bibi was getting anxious.

As Topher let Ka out of her basket, he heard Ellie asking Sanjit to come round as soon as he could to make plans for the next couple of days. They'd already decided they wanted to go to the Museum of London one day and the Science Museum on the other, but not where they were going first. When they'd had supper and Sanjit still hadn't come round, Topher rang his mobile and learned he couldn't get away that day.

'And I'll be lucky to get away tomorrow,' Sanjit groaned, 'and if I do I won't be able to move. My auntie is insisting I eat a mountain of food and worst of all, Bibi is testing me on my knowledge of the Gurus.'

Topher could hear the hubbub of Punjabi voices in the background. It sounded like one big family reunion, noisier even than the Wentworths.

But Sanjit did manage to get away. He arrived at half past nine next morning, looking as trendy as ever. To get away from Luke and Russell they went up to the roof terrace on the second floor, where the boys weren't allowed. It looked south over the rooftops of North London, as far the Post Office tower. Ellie tossed a coin.

'Heads the Science Museum today. Tails the MOL.'

'Heads!' yelled Sanjit.

'Tails!' Topher was into Science too, but he couldn't help thinking about Ingwar the Boneless and thought he might find out a bit more. The MOL showed you what London was like from prehistoric times right up to the present day and it was sure to have a Viking bit. Tails won and they set off. Topher didn't bother asking Ka if she wanted to come with them. He remembered her reaction when he'd mentioned the Viking leader's name. Instead, he left her curled up on his bed with Duo, one of the kittens she'd had soon after she came back from her Roman trip.

Sanjit joshed with Topher as they hurried to Archway tube station.

'Museums! All that old-fashioned stuff. Why?'

'Because he is old fashioned?' Ellie laughed.

But when they got on the tube they all quietened down. There were policemen on the train and they all remembered how there had nearly been a terrorist attack on this very line. A young man had planned to set off a bomb, killing and injuring loads of people. Just the thought of being trapped underground in total darkness was scary. The thought of being burned alive was horrific. The bomber had carried the bomb in his rucksack. Some people still carried rucksacks and briefcases and shopping bags, but Topher noted how things had changed since he used to live in London. Then, people on the underground never looked at each other. They used to read books or newspapers or stare straight up at the tube map. There had been signs warning people to be on the lookout for suspicious packages, but no one seemed to take much notice of them. Now there were even more warning signs and people were obeying them. Their eyes were all over the place and, it seemed to Topher, often came to rest on Asian-looking people. They stared at Sanjit, though he wasn't carrying a rucksack or any other sort of bag. He hadn't even brought a waterproof, though the weather forecast was for showers. It was a relief for all of them to reach Moorgate Station and leave the tube, especially when they got into the open air.

The Museum was good – even Sanjit said it was – but Topher didn't find what he wanted. In fact the section on Anglo-Saxons and Vikings was a bit sparse, not half as good as the Roman bit where you could walk down a real Roman street. There was only one Anglo-Saxon house with a thatched roof, and that was only a reconstruction, because none of the real ones had survived. Ellie and Sanjit took a quick look, and went off to find something more interesting. Topher hung back and did the Viking bit by himself. There wasn't much of that either, but he did discover that Ragnar Lothbrok, he of the hairy britches – Ingwar's dad! – led at least one raid on Londonwic as they called it then. Topher was looking at a glass case full of Viking swords and spears and gruesome axe-heads, when Ellie and Sanjit reappeared.

'Come *on*.' Ellie grabbed his arm. 'There's loads of better stuff in the other rooms.'

'Like beautiful girlie dresses,' said Sanjit.

'And whipping posts for bad boys like you,' said Ellie, as they entered a Victorian street, where there was one in the middle of a squalid cobbled square. But Ellie most wanted to show Topher an advert.

'For Signor Cappelli's Learned Cats!' She read it out. '"They can beat a drum, turn a spit, grind knives, strike upon an anvil and roast coffee. And the cleverest of the company will draw water out of a well at her master's command." And you think Ka's clever!'

'She is. Cleverer in fact.'

The others laughed and he thought about Ka and hoped she would be there when he got back to Ellie's. Suddenly he longed to see her, but when they got back in the afternoon, she wasn't.

Chapter 5

'What's up?' Ellie, on the way to her room, saw Topher staring at his bed. She didn't notice the statue, half hidden by the folds of the blue duvet.

'Ka's gone.'

'So?' She studied his face. 'What's wrong with that? You didn't expect her to stay there all day, did you?'

He didn't say anything. She wouldn't understand. He picked a few of Ka's hairs from the bed where he'd last seen her curled up with Duo.

Ellie said, 'She's probably downstairs with Duo, or in the garden. Let's go and look.'

He shook his head and she exploded. 'Sometimes you're so negative, Topher! You're worried, but you won't do anything to help. Hopeless, that's what you should be called!'

It wasn't fair.

Later he heard her calling Ka from the garden. He kept an eye on the statue, which he'd put beside his bed, but it stayed dull and still. And she noticed it when she came back to his room to apologise for losing her temper.

She said, 'Isn't it risky bringing that? Your dad would go mad if you lost it.'

I didn't bring it. The words stayed on the tip of his tongue.

*

The statue was still there in the morning. He'd had a rotten night, waking up often to see if anything was happening. When he did set off with the others for the Archway tube station he felt tired and anxious. They went via Arburton Road, where Topher used to live, to see if Ka was there – Ellie insisted – but of course she wasn't. It all looked very familiar – the terraced houses, the plane trees with their patchy trunks, the pigeons cooing on the chimney tops, several cats, even the dog barking madly at the window of Number 33. But when Ellie knocked on the door of Number 35 to ask the new residents, the woman who answered said she hadn't seen a cat answering Ellie's description. Topher didn't say, 'I told you so' but he did try to cheer himself up with positive thoughts. So far Ka had always returned from her travels, usually safe and sound. As they walked along he listened to Sanjit cracking jokes, but when they got to the end of the underpass, leading to the tube station, his pessimism returned. Police officers guarded the entrance, and they were armed. A billboard said it was because of a bomb scare on the Northern Line.

Suddenly going anywhere seemed like a bad idea.

'Let's give up and go home,' he said, and Ellie sighed dramatically.

'There are bomb scares all the time, Topher. This is London. And there *are* buses you know, and taxis. Where there's a will ... '

'Okay, okay.' She was right of course. They could see the tops of buses going along the Archway Road. To forestall a lecture he agreed to take one. 'If that's okay with you, Sanjit?'

To his disappointment – he *really* didn't want to go – Sanjit shrugged. So they set off to the bus stop, where Ellie consulted the timetable and made notes. As they waited for her to work out which buses to take to get to Kensington, Topher noticed Sanjit looking worried.

'What are you thinking, mate?'

'About when that bomber couldn't get on a tube, some time back, so he caught the bus.'

'So was I.'

The bus arrived, a red double-decker.

'Ellie, forget it.' They said it together, but she stepped onto the platform.

'I hear what you say, guys, but I'm going even if you're not. Lightning doesn't strike twice, you know, not in the same place.'

'Scientifically speaking, that isn't true,' said Sanjit, but he stepped on too, and so, nervously, did Topher.

While they queued to buy tickets, he and Sanjit discussed safety tactics – to Ellie's obvious disgust. She started to go upstairs but the boys decided that down-stairs, just inside the door, was the safest place. From there they could watch everyone who got on and they could get off easily if they had to. Well, quite easily. The bus did have automatic doors operated by the driver.

'Would we tell the driver or ring the bell?' said Sanjit.

Ellie pointed to a notice saying 'Do not speak to the driver when the bus is moving'.

'I think it'd be permitted in an emergency,' Topher replied sarcastically, but Ellie still looked scornful. 'How can you spot a suicide bomber? They don't wear badges.'

It was a good question. They all sat down near the front, and as the bus stopped and started and people got on Topher thought about it more and more. A bomber had to have somewhere to hide the bomb, like a rucksack or a case or a shopping bag. And didn't some bombers strap bombs round their middles? Luckily it was a summer day and quite hot so most people were lightly dressed. You could tell that most of them weren't hiding bulky objects under their clothes. You could also eliminate skinny girls with bare midriffs and bare-chested men in tight jeans – if they weren't carrying bags or big packages. But how big was big? How big was a bomb? And could you tell from a person's facial expression what he or she was going to do? A lot of people looked tense and worried and several were sweating. Was it the heat or nerves?

It took three buses to get to Kensington and seemed to take forever. But at last they were on the final one, another double-decker, and Ellie said, 'Not long now. We're in the Brompton Road. It's one or maybe two more stops.'

It was getting hotter. Topher could feel sweat on his forehead. They passed Harrods and were coming up to the Victoria and Albert Museum when the bus stopped again. But as he stood up, Ellie shook her head. 'Not this one. The next.'

The queue at this stop was quite long – eight people in all – and first in line was a woman in a burka. Topher felt himself go tense as she stepped on. All you could see were her eyes and the toes of a pair of trainers. How could you be sure it was a woman? Or that she wasn't hiding a bomb? Ellie sighed heavily. She was sitting next to him in the seat by the window and he could read her mind. *You're being prejudiced, Topher.* The woman bought a ticket from the driver who wore a purple turban, and walked heavily to the back seat. She moved slowly as if she was pregnant. There were six more people in the queue, seven if you counted a baby in a buggy – and of course you had to. Was it really a baby? Topher peered into the buggy as the mother paid – and the baby started to cry. Definitely a baby, but there was still room in the buggy for a bomb. The mother, a large black lady, glared at Topher, then settled in the seat on the other side of the gangway, squashing Sanjit against the window. A black girl in shorts and skimpy T-shirt went upstairs. There was no way she could be hiding anything. She was the only one of the eight new boarders who looked beyond suspicion.

Topher turned to scan the lower deck. It was full now. A white man in a business suit, carrying a chunkier than average briefcase, flashed a bus pass at the driver and went upstairs. So did the brown-skinned woman behind him. She also looked as if she might be pregnant – or carrying a bomb round her middle. The Japanese couple behind her both had rucksacks. They went upstairs too.

Then came a man with a bushy beard carrying a bag. Last came a middle-aged woman carrying a bulky Harrods bag. She glared at Topher as if to say, you ought to give me your seat, and he was thinking he might, when the driver said, 'There's room upstairs,' and she heaved herself onto the lower step.

With a ring of the bell the driver pulled out. The bus gathered speed and then stopped for traffic lights – and Topher, turning to look behind him, saw someone in the middle of the back seat, fumbling with a bag at his feet. He froze for a second – the man might be looking for a book or iPod – then heard himself yelling, 'Open the door!' as he jumped out of his seat and leaned hard on the bell in front of him.

A Harrods bag came tumbling down the stairs.

Ellie grabbed his arm.

Topher banged on the Perspex wall surrounding the driver. 'BOMB! There's a BOMB! Open the doors!'

He pointed to the back of the bus where the man – it was the one with a beard – was still delving in the bag. But the doors didn't open.

'Get out. GET OUT EVERYONE!' He shouted as loud as he could and heard someone say, 'Probably a hoax.' But other people were standing up. The man at the back was sitting upright now and staring straight ahead. But then he glanced down at his bag and Topher saw a wisp of white smoke curling out of it.

'BOMB!' Topher jabbed his finger at the man, and a man near him stood up. Several people nearby stood up and moved to the front of the bus. Now there was an acrid smell, and Sanjit – he must have climbed over the large woman – was by the driver saying something in Punjabi.

At last – it seemed to take ages – the doors started to wheeze open, slowly, too slowly, as the driver spoke into a mobile.

Sanjit yelled, 'Get out!' in English and then again in Punjabi and again in English.

And now people surged forward, blocking Topher's exit. He felt bodies pressing him sideways, back against the driver's cab, as people from the back of the bus surged forward. More people bundled down the stairs causing a jam, trapping him in a corner. People pushed past him. But they couldn't all get through the door. The space wasn't big enough. Then, at last it was. The doors were fully open. The crush eased a bit but he still couldn't get out. Through a gap he thought he saw Ellie on the pavement, but then the gap closed again. More and more people were pushing by him. But the crowd was getting thinner. Now he could see the back of the bus and the man with the bag, making no attempt to move. Framed by his bushy beard, pink lips opened and closed and white teeth flashed. Then – BANG! – the bus shook and the man at the back rose into the air. Crash! His head hit the ceiling. Then he started to descend, till he hit the floor and crumpled into a pool of yellow sticky stuff.

'Topher!' He recognised Ellie's voice and turned to see her on the pavement screaming. 'Come out!'

'Move, lad!'

He couldn't move.

Couldn't think straight.

People on the pavement were shouting.

Hands were pulling at him.

Then he was on the pavement with railings in front of them. He saw leaves poking through the railings. He saw a Coca-Cola can stuck between them. There were people either side of him pulling him sideways.

'Come on, lad. Let's get away from here.'

'The park,' one of them said. 'That would be safer. Where's the gate?'

As whoever they were pulled him along he saw broken glass at his feet. He heard it crunch. Glancing up he saw glassless windows in the side of the bus. He heard vehicles hooting and drivers shouting.

One yelled, 'The lights have changed!'

Everything's changed, he thought. My life has changed. Then he was dragged in another direction and there was grass under his feet and someone was telling him to sit and wait. Hands pushed him down onto a low wall bordering a flowerbed. He sat. He waited. Far off he heard a siren blaring. Then a large black bird, an enormous black bird, jumped out from behind a bush.

'Caw!' It walked towards him and stopped.

'Caw!' Its orange eyes looked straight into his. Its dagger beak was level with his throat. But it wasn't a gigantic bird. He knew that straightaway because he had a sense of déjà vu. He had shrunk, he realised as the bird turned and spread its shiny tail feathers in front of him. It was happening again. He was going time-travelling.

33

Ka! She was his first thought. *I'm coming to find you!*

Eagerly he climbed onto the bird's back, grasping its springy tail feathers with his hands. He felt the barbules parting as he clambered up, but they held firm. When he reached the top the bird lifted its tail, tipping him into the hollow of its shiny back. Landing on his stomach, it took him a while to catch his breath and get into a kneeling position. He was sliding from side to side as the bird stepped from one clawed foot to another as if impatient to be off. But he managed to grasp the bird's neck with both hands and steady himself. And he wasn't frightened, for the bird's springy feathers felt familiar and he was filled with excitement, as the bird tensed and broke into a run, its ragged wings flapping furiously. He felt a surge of energy beneath him as the bird left the ground.

Up up up it went, wings whooshing.

Up up up, diagonally across the park, which was suddenly a square of green below. Up up up, with the wind pulling at his clothes as blue lights flashed in the streets below. Ambulances, police cars and fire engines were rushing through the streets to the exploded bus. But he couldn't hear the sirens. He couldn't hear the roar of traffic. All he could hear was the bird's wings whooshing as they beat up and down.

Below him was a London like Legoland, but soon the buildings were smaller even than Lego as the bird flew higher and higher. Vehicles racing through the streets were like beetles, then ants. The river Thames looked like a silver ribbon and then a thread. And soon he couldn't see the streets, buildings or even the river. Briefly, he saw the triangle of islands that was Great Britain, then only the bulky shapes of the world's continents surrounded by blue. Then, even they faded as he entered a realm of stars, some shooting past him, others exploding, others whirling, all so dazzling in their brilliance that he closed his eyes to rest them from the glare. And then he must have slept – as the bird flew through space and time and dimensions he couldn't name – for when he opened his eyes he was somewhere he didn't recognise.

Chapter 6

Quickly he closed his eyes again, for there were scraps of what seemed like a dream in his head. He'd been on a bird's back flying through the star-filled heavens with comets and shooting stars flying past. It was a brilliant, exciting dream and he kept his eyes tightly shut, trying to hold on to it, but the more he tried, the more rapidly the pictures faded. Going, going, gone. After a few moments he couldn't even remember what he was trying to hold on to – and there was something pricking his face.

Sitting up and opening his eyes he saw corn stubble – that's what was pricking him – and dark brown earth, and sheaves of yellow corn, dotted among the short stalks. He was in the middle of a cornfield, no not in the middle, but near the hedge which surrounded the field. He was under a tree in full leaf. And yes, now he remembered, he was supposed to be scaring birds away from the corn. That's why he was there. So why had he fallen asleep? He started to panic. Had anyone noticed? He'd be in trouble if anyone had. And where were the other boys? He remembered now, the whole tithing, all ten boys had been in the field with him. Haegel had sent them to keep birds off the corn, for the village needed every grain to keep them in flour through the winter.

Now he listened for laughter, suspecting a trick. He braced himself for a shock if one of the boys jumped out – from behind a sheaf of corn, or out of the hedge, or even dropped out of a tree. They must be hiding somewhere. Listening for laughter he started to look, scanning the field again. There seemed to be no one else about, but the others must be here somewhere. They couldn't have been gone long, for there weren't any birds either, well only one, a raven he thought, high in the sky. For a moment his dream flickered in his head. Gone. Hadn't there been a raven in that? Forgetting for a moment that he now worshipped the God of the Cross, he watched the bird soar, and gave thanks to Woden, for sending it to scare away the crows. Then a loud mewing brought him back to earth.

'Mia-OW!'

'Ka!' He remembered his cat. An excellent bird scarer, he had brought her to the field with him. So where was she?

'Ka!' He called her name but she didn't come running as she usually did.

'Mia-OW!' She sounded fraught. Was she stuck in a tree? Surely not, she was far too clever for that.

'Mia-OW!'

Had she got herself caught in a fowler's trap? Trap! Suddenly his mind was working fast. Had *he* been trapped? Why had he fallen asleep? Why was he alone? Where were the other boys? They'd been getting at him a lot lately, but he'd left the village with them that morning. He remembered crossing the river in the skiff, and Ka had been with them, and – yes – Cadgael had joked about sacrificing her. Sacrificing the Corn Cat was an old pagan custom. They didn't do it any more now they were Christians. Well, not with a real cat. But Cadgael had wondered aloud how their pagan ancestors had managed to bind the cat to the last sheaf of corn so it couldn't get away. 'Let's try!' Aelfred and Alfmaer had made a grab for Ka. They hadn't caught her but the skiff had rocked, and Cadgael had laughed, though he was supposed to keep them in order. Well, they were all supposed to keep each other in order. That's how the tithing worked, but Cadgael was the thane's son, so the others, the sons of mere carls, tended to follow his lead.

Topher glanced at the huge arching sky, blue like a blackbird's egg with only a few wisps of cloud. The sun was almost overhead, so it was past noon. Had he eaten? Yes – and Ka had gone to sleep in the basket they'd brought the bread in, while they ate and drank ale. He remembered feeling sleepy, as if he'd had too much ale, though he never slept during the day. Only old folk did that – unless . . . His suspicions grew.

'Mia-OOW!' Ka sounded frantic.

'Don't worry. I'll find you!'

He listened intently. Where was her cry coming from? Suddenly full of foreboding, he headed for the middle of the field. That's where the last sheaf of corn had been placed, ready for the harvest festival. The straw image of the Corn Cat had been hidden inside it, for it was

38

Haligmonath, the month when crops were gathered and offerings made to the gods. God, he reminded himself as he stumbled over the rough ground, there was only one God who had died on the cross.

As he approached the middle of the field his suspicions grew, for the cries got louder. The middle sheaf. That was where they were coming from.

'I'm coming, Ka!'

But as he reached it, boys sprang from behind the hedge at the top end of the field. Filling the opening to the next field, they started to race towards him hurling sticks and stones and clods of earth.

'Let be! Let be! Leave the sheaf alone!'

But Topher carried on pulling it apart.

'Leave it alone!' The boys raced down the slope.

Topher ripped away handfuls of straw.

Baying like hounds, they yelled, 'Stop! Stop!'

But he could see the basket buried in the straw.

They got closer.

He wrenched at the basket. Got it. Pulled at the lid. But it wouldn't come off.

'Leave it! Leave it there!' The boys were bearing down on him waving sticks.

A clod of earth hit the back of his head.

'Sorry, Ka. You'll have to stay inside.' He began to run, the basket swinging from his hand. The other boys were getting closer. Best keep running. As fast as he could. Poor Ka, but at least the baying had stopped. He glanced over his shoulder. Had Cadgael thought better of it? No, he was in front and the others were still following, silent now, putting all their strength into running.

But the river was nearly in reach. He could see the reeds lining the bank, but the settlement was on the other side of the river, that was the trouble. He would have to cross it. But first he must splash through the water meadow. Try not to sink. Then hope he could find the skiff hidden in the reeds. Here was the meadow now. There were the cows, hock deep in mud. He ran as fast as he could, as lightly as he could, trying to tread on the grassy sods and miss the mud between them. Curses! Slipping, he felt mud sucking his leather shoe. Out again. Schluck. But now his breath was coming in hoarse gasps, and he had a stitch in his side, sharp as a knife. But he kept going. Had to. Had to. Had to.

Ka was silent.

He reached the bank.

Where, where was the skiff?

There, tied to some tall reeds. Putting the basket in first, he pulled the boat into the water. Then he jumped in, grabbed the paddle and headed for the opposite bank, with Cadgael's shouts in his ears.

Chapter 7

Safe for a few minutes at least, he looked back. Good. Some of the other boys were stuck in the mud, and others had stopped to help, but not Cadgael. He'd left them behind, and seemed to glide over the meadow, his long fair hair streaming behind him, as he made long leaps. When he reached the bank he picked up a handful of mud.

'Come back, Topher!'

The mud landed in the water.

Topher tried to comfort Ka, still silent in the basket. 'You're safe now. I'll let you out as soon as I can.'

Cadgael threw more mud. That missed too. It just made ripples in the water. Then he cupped his hands round his mouth and hollered, 'Spoilsport! It was just a bit of fun!'

Un–un–un. The word resounded over the water.

'Don't you go tittle-tattling!'

Ing-ing-ing!

'Or I will!'

Ill-ill-ill!

The threat was obvious. You tell on us, we'll tell on you. Now Topher remembered the downside of being in the tithing. It wasn't just being in a gang and having good sport together. It was keeping each other in line. *You are all responsible for each other's behaviour.*

That's what Haegel had said at the joining meet. *If one of you, any of you does wrong, all of you will be blamed. All of you will be punished. It is good practice for when you join an adult tithing. We must all keep an eye on one another. We must help each other keep the law. If anyone breaks the law, the rest of the tithing must bring the lawbreaker before the court. If they don't they will all be punished.*

As Topher steered the skiff through the water he tried to think. What would happen if he ran home and told his father the other boys had tried to sacrifice Ka? He heard Topheric's voice in his head. 'Where's your proof, son?' He spoke Saxon with a Danish lilt, sometimes missing the harder sounds.

He heard his mother's clearer voice. 'Did you gainsay them, Topher?'

Had he tried to argue the others out of it? How could he when he was asleep? Why had he fallen asleep? He'd only once slept during the day, and that was when he'd had a bad pain and his mother had given him a sleeping draught. Could someone have slipped a sleeping herb into his drink? He stopped rowing for a moment. What would Haegel say if he told him what had happened? Would Cadgael deny it or tell the truth? What would the other boys say, and who would Haegel believe?

'Mwow!'

'All right, Ka.' He pulled on the oars again, for even if he didn't stay on the other side, he must take her to safety. Soon he heard ducks quacking in the reeds, and then more noises from the settlement merged with the splashing of his paddle – squealing pigs and crowing roosters and the steady hack of axes chopping wood, for there was always someone chopping wood in the village.

'Not long now, Ka.'

As soon as he'd tied up the skiff, he tried to get the lid off her basket, but it was bound with leather thongs and the knots were tight. Some jest. Someone had wanted to make sure Ka couldn't escape. Someone wanted Ka to burn. He could still hear shouts from the other side of the river, where the other boys were stranded, if he didn't return. Too bad. Free at last, Ka leaped onto dry land and Topher saw Beric, the basket maker, sitting outside the hut where he dried the rushes. To Topher's surprise the man beckoned him over.

'Come on, Ka. You're safe now.'

But she didn't go with him to see what Beric wanted. She set off up the slope towards the thatched home-steads at the top.

'Good day, Beric.'

The basket maker was a quiet, mild-mannered man, who didn't have much to say to people, even when they came to barter for one of his baskets. But now he seemed keen to know what had been going on.

'What was all that hollering about, lad?' His eyes were curtained by yellow stringy hair, but he spotted the basket. 'And what are you doing with Aethelwith's basket?'

So that's whom it belonged to. Useful.

'I'm returning it to her. The others asked me to,' he lied – God forgive him. Then he left before there were more questions. How odd, he thought, that Beric was Sigeric's father. They neither looked nor sounded like each other. Sigeric was small and dark haired and always jabbering, often bad-mouthing folk – and he moved suddenly like a grasshopper. Beric was very still, except for his long fingers which never stopped plaiting reeds or willow wands.

He caught Ka up. 'What do you think?'

She stopped beside a field where two men were leaning stooks of barley against each other. *Ca...rrre...ful. Ca...rrrre...ful.*

'Of Sigeric?' he spoke softly so the men wouldn't hear him. 'Of course. Was he the one who wanted to burn you?'

Be...rrric. Be...rrric.

'Beric wanted to burn you?'

She gave him one of her hard stares, her 'don't be silly' look, her eyes like amber in the sunlight, then set off again. When they reached the wicket fence, she jumped onto it and over to the other side. Topher opened the gate and closed it. Then they both ran towards Haegel's homestead in the middle, past another homestead where a woman was sitting in the doorway carding wool as her children played five stones. Past the blacksmith flattening a length of molten metal, with ringing blows, making sparks fly. Then they were at Haegel's homestead, a group of thatched buildings with wattle walls, but was Haegel at home? From inside the

44

hall, the largest building, he could hear Cadwynn, Cadgael's mother, ordering serfs around, and through the doorway, he could see them moving benches around. It looked as if they were getting the hall ready for something. Haegel's hall was where the whole village gathered for important meetings, so perhaps he had something important to say or maybe a scop had arrived? An evening of storytelling would be good.

'What do you want, Topher?' Cadwynn had come to the door, but luckily didn't wait for an answer, as a child inside started bawling. Good, for now he wasn't sure what to say. And now someone else was calling him.

'Topher!' Oh no, it was Aethelwith, Aethelstan's mother, standing by her loom in the doorway of her house. 'W-where's Aethelstan? Why have you got my basket?'

The blacksmith stopped banging. Aethelstan's sisters stopped playing five stones and stared at him. Aethelwith tugged on a plait of her hair. They all thought something had happened to Aethelstan. Why else would Topher come home alone?

He called out, 'Aethelstan's all right. He's in Top Field with the others!' and hurried over.

'Then why are you not with them?' Aethelwith grabbed the basket. 'And who made this hole?'

Oh dear. There was a hole. Ka must have tried to scratch her way out.

'And why have you left Top Field before sunset?' Aethelwith went on and on. 'You're a lazy boy, Topher. If I were your mother...'

But she stopped when she heard her loom weights clicking, and saw Ka patting the weights, twisting the warp threads together.

'Shoo, cat! Don't ruin my weaving too!' She clapped her hands and they both escaped.

But now Topher wondered what to do. Should he go home? Was that the right thing to do? If he did there would be more questions. He stopped to think about it, for his family's homestead was the next one. Their living house was in the corner of the village near the boundary fence. It stood out because it was built in the Danish way, from logs. Whole tree-trunks split lengthways stood side by side, buttressed on the outside so there was no need of supporting posts inside. He could see his grandmother tending the beehives. Perhaps it would be best to return to Top Field before she saw him? He needed to think.

'But you stay here, Ka. Go on.'

She rubbed round his legs, reluctant to leave him despite her ordeal.

'No.' He shooed her away. 'It's you I came back for. Go home. Ask Mother for some milk and find somewhere to sleep for the rest of the day. Keep out of harm's way.'

When he returned to Top Field the other boys greeted him with scornful laughter.

'So you've come back?' Cadgael looked worried.

'I took the basket back to Aethelstan's mother's.'

'And...?'

They all looked anxious to know what Topher had told her.

'She was angry because Ka had scratched a hole in it. She wanted to know who had put her in it.'

'And?' Cadgael's blue eyes bored into him.

Aethelstan was standing behind him, red-faced, biting his bottom lip.

'I told her I didn't know how, but that we all, the whole tithing, decided that it should be returned to her forthwith.'

May God forgive him for telling a string of lies.

Cadgael said, 'Did you tell her you fell asleep when you were supposed to be keeping crows off the corn?'

'No.'

'Then we will not tell her – or anyone – if you don't tell them of our jest.'

'Jest, is that what you call it?'

'Yes, it was a jest. We would not have burned the cat.'

'We are not pagans, even if you are, Topher, son of Topheric,' said Sigeric, Beric's son.

'I am not a pagan. I believe in the God of the Cross.'

'But your Viking father doesn't.' Sigeric again.

'He does, and he isn't a Viking!'

They were the usual jibes.

Topheric, Topher's father, had come to Haegellisdom as a Danish trader many years ago, but he stayed to marry Gytha, Topher's mother, who was an Anglo-Saxon. The priest had joined them together. They all lived as Christians and his father was well thought of. At the last moot the elders had voted him onto their council. He was not a Viking. Vikings were Danes who robbed and killed.

Topher said, 'In our family we all worship the God of the Cross.'

'Then why do you have a shrine to Freya in your sleeping house, sleepy boy?' Sigeric was determined to stir things up.

'We don't!'

But this was all going wrong. He'd meant to say, 'I will not tell on you, that you tried to sacrifice Ka, if you promise never to harm her again.'

Why did Cadgael always get the upperhand? Because his father was a thane, and his was a carl? Why did Sigeric have it in for him? Because his father was not on the council?

'Sleepy boy! Sleepy boy!' Sigeric jumped around like a frog.

Cadgael said, 'Shut up, Sigeric.' He flung an arm round Topher's shoulders. 'We are blood brothers, remember, and we stick together, all of us.'

It is true that at the tithing meet they had all scored their arms on the blade of a spear. They'd sworn an oath of loyalty and mingled blood. But . . .

'Come!' Cadgael called the others, who stepped forward and linked arms in a circle.

They stamped their feet and chanted that they were brothers, and they looked like brothers, most of them, with their fair hair and light skin. They all wore short cyrtles dyed brown or blue or green. But Topher, even though he looked like them, felt awkward and alone.

Chapter 8

For the rest of the day the boys were friendly enough, and in the evening they all returned to the village at sunset. There was room in the skiff for five at the most, so they had to make three crossings. Topher waited in the last group with Cadgael as Aethelstan rowed back to get them. They watched Haegel on the opposite bank. There was no mistaking Cadgael's father, the village headman, for he was so tall, even without his mane of braided hair. But not as tall as my father, Topher couldn't help thinking. Cadgael, a smaller image of his father, said, 'I wonder why my father is there and what he has said, that they all run to the hall instead of back to their own homesteads.'

Sigeric had run straight past his father's reed-drying hut by the river and his living house just inside the gate.

Topher said, 'I think a scop may have come. Your mother was telling serfs to get the moot hall ready when I took Ka back.'

And when Aethelstan reached the bank he confirmed Topher's hunch.

It was getting dark, when they reached the other side, but a harvest moon, round and pink, hung over the settlement.

Haegel called out, 'Is all the grain safe?'

'Yes, Father!'

'Then hurry to the moot hall.' Haegel held the skiff steady. 'You will eat there tonight. But mind, lads, you must still be up before the birds tomorrow. No sleeping in. It's not a bad job though, is it, bird scaring? I remember it well. You can play noisy games and the birds keep well away. Did you play Saxons and Vikings or kick-ball? Oh, I need not ask.' Spotting the pig's bladder under Cadgael's arm, he took it and kicked so that it went arching over the boundary fence.

The hall was nearly full. It looked as if the whole village, nearly a hundred people, were crammed inside. Some sat at the edges on timber platforms padded with sheepskins. Others sat on benches. Serfs and children sat on the floor, looking up at the red-haired scop, already on the dais at the far end of the room. On the wall behind him, rush lights flickered in the darkness and his shadow danced as he strummed, filling the room with the liquid notes of the lyre. Cadgael went to the front and sat down with his younger brothers and sister.

'Over here, Topher!'

At first Topher didn't see his father, it was so dark on the other side of the hall. Then he saw Topheric's hair shining red like copper in the glow of a rush light, and made his way over to where his family was gathered. They might not be the richest or highest born family, but they were the best looking, he couldn't help thinking. His father, a head taller than all the other men, had broad shoulders and a strong handsome face. He was sitting on the side platform. Arrow, his black and white dog, was at his feet. Grandmother, Mother's grey-haired mother, sat beside him with Emric, his younger sister, on her lap. Aemer, his other sister, leaned against her legs and Grandmother was combing her long fair hair. Both sisters were in their nightshifts, ready to be carried to bed if they fell asleep before the entertainment was over.

'Here you are, son.' Gytha handed Topher a platter of cold meat and a hunk of bread. She was wearing her best blue dress, the colour of harebells which matched her eyes. The amber glass beads that Father had brought from Jutland hung between her bronze shoulder brooches.

'Here. Wash it down with this.' Topheric handed Topher a beaker of ale, as he settled on the floor beside Arrow. It was good to feel the dog's warmth against his thigh, his father's legs strong against his back. The scop was about to begin. There were rush lights round him now. The smith had just put them there, in stands he'd made, so they could all see the scop's lean, expressive face.

'Lo, praise of the prowess of people-kings
Of spear-armed Dane in days long sped ... '

The room fell silent as he began. Beowulf. It was one of Topher's favourite stories, and the scop told it well, carrying the listeners over the waves, with his rich northern burr and dancing hands, lifting his voice so they saw the waves as high as houses and heard them crashing against the ship as the brave warrior sailed north to the land of the Vikings. Then they saw the monster, Grendel, waiting for him on the shore, lying

51

low, licking his lips – and as the scop licked his lips they feared for their hero, till they saw him again, sword shining in his hands. He was ready for the monster, he was ready for anything and soon the fight began!

Topher could hardly breathe as the battle raged. Now Beowulf was winning, but then Grendel was winning. Then Beowulf was fighting back, but so was the monster. The battle raged for days and days. Willing the hero to win, Topher thought he might burst, he feared for him so much, then – Phew! – at last the blood of Grendel spewed onto the sand. A flood of blood reddened the shore and he breathed again. The whole room gasped with relief. But not for long. The scop's face grew grim. For here came another foe, the monster's mother! Topher felt his sinews tighten as she came to wreak revenge for the death of her son. Could Beowulf defeat her too? Could he summon the strength to fight again? Could he find the skill? Of course! With courage and cunning Beowulf defeated her too! But it still wasn't over. There was yet another foe, another fight, this time with a fearful dragon, and the flickering torches burnt low before the hero triumphed again, to be rewarded with gold rings and glistening treasure.

For a few moments the room was silent, for everyone, young and old, was in the land of long ago with Beowulf. Then, as they returned to the present, the room heaved with a collective 'Aaah!'

That story always went down well.

'Those Danes couldn't have done it without Beowulf,' said a voice from the darkness. 'Eh, Topheric?'

Topheric laughed. ''Course not!'

He always took their jibes in good part. They all knew he had been a Danish trader till a storm had wrecked his boat and thrown him onto Saxon shores.

'Hit and run, that's what Danes do,' said another voice. Topher didn't know whose.

'Better at running!' sneered a voice he recognised but couldn't place.

'I'd have let Grendel eat the lot of them!' said a woman and the room filled with laughter.

A drinking horn, filled with mead, passed from man to man and to some of the women. Haegel's wife, Cadwynn, went to the dais and offered a brimming flask of ale to the scop, who threw back his head and drained it dry.

'Well,' Haegel laughed. 'Storytelling is thirsty work, but let's have another tale before we go to the sleeping house.'

'I'll sing this one,' said the scop. He handed Haegel the empty flask, and the hall went quiet as he plucked the strings of his lyre.

'I'll tell you a tale that you all should heed,
Of a Viking most horrid in look and in deed,

Ingwar the Boneless is his horrid name,
Gristly grim issue of his mother's shame.'

Benches creaked as the company settled in their seats, but Topher felt his father's legs stiffen.

'King Ragnar, his father, so hairy his britches
   He couldn't keep in them, so fierce were his itches.'

A funny story. Even better. The company laughed and
relaxed in their seats. But not Topheric. Topher felt him
tense as if he was going to stand up.

'And he sailed to England across the North Sea
With Ingwar the Boneless and his brothers three.

They pillaged and plundered wherever they went,
Heads of Northumbrians they smote and they dent.

Ingwar though boneless fought with great rage
For his long limp body was held up by a cage.

His arms were so strong they could kill with one stroke.
Over many an enemy the raven did croak.

But then good King Aella caught bad King Ragnar,
Took off his britches and threw them afar.

And then he threw Ragnar into a deep pit
Where by poisonous snakes, he was deeply bit.

Writhing in pain Ragnar called on his son
To take bloody revenge for what Aella had done.

And Ingwar swore that he certainly would
Make Aella suffer as much as he could.

But he bided his time for that was his style
And pretended to be Aella's friend for a while.

He took land as wergild for his father's life
And when Aella was sleeping he sharpened his knife.

When Aella turned over he sliced open his back
Then from his chest his two lungs he did hack.

He spread them like wings, one lung on each side
And writhing with pain the good King then died.

Then he took Aella's land and called himself King.
'I may not have bones but I'm not a weakling!'

Then ominous words came from Ingwar's big mouth,
'I've conquered the north, now I'm heading south.'

As he finished Staneric sprang to his feet, waving
the drinking horn. 'Let him come here! We'll be ready
for him!'

The others laughed, but Topheric said, 'Listen!
There's more.'

And he was right. Rippling the strings with his long
fingers, the scop began to sing again, and it seemed to
Topher that as he did, he looked straight at him. His eyes
looked into his and as he sang, a muscle in his pale cheek
twitched.

'There will come a hero with a torn hem,

55

He'll help but won't stop these very bad men.

So laugh if you wish, friends, but heed what I say,
Ingwar the Boneless is coming this way.

Is coming this way...Is coming this way...'

With a ripple of notes he finished, but as the company clapped and cheered and stamped their feet, Topheric stood up and spoke to his wife.

'Gytha, take the children home to bed, for I must speak to that man, and so must Haegel and the elders.' Calling out, 'You, scop, wait!' he crossed the room, for the man was leaving the hall with Beric.

Someone said, 'Who do you think you are?'

And Haegel blocked the doorway. 'I am headman here, Topheric. Let the man go to his bed. He has travelled all day and entertained us all night. He is tired. Why do you want him?'

'Because he is warning us. What he says is true. Last year, I heard a Danish trader say a heathen horde would head south and this adds strength to that story.'

Haegel laughed. 'Exactly! A story. The man was telling a story, Topheric.'

'A true story, Haegel. I remember those names from when I lived with the Danes. Ingwar and his brothers could well have done all that the scop said. They are not content with holding Northumbria. They want Mercia too and East Engleland and Wessex. They want the whole country. They have Yorvik. I heard they had

56

sacked Snotengahan and Hreathandune, two towns in Mercia. They burned them to the ground and they could be on their way to do the same here.'

'In the morning then,' said Haegel, looking more serious. 'For you mean well. I know that. We will talk to him together. Tonight he is staying in Beric's sleeping house, for he has room since his wife passed to the Other Place. I will send someone to tell Beric we wish to speak with our guest before he leaves.'

Though it was much later than usual when he went to the sleeping house, Topher couldn't get to sleep. He couldn't get the scop's words out of his head. So he lay awake, his sisters sleeping either side of him. His father couldn't sleep either. Topher could hear him murmuring to his mother on the other side of the sleeping house. He couldn't hear what they said because the bed curtain muffled the sound, but he could guess. He thought his grandmother was awake too, in her corner of the room, because he couldn't hear her snores. But he could hear and feel Ka's purrs as she lay in the curl of his stomach, under the covers.

'What do you think, Ka?'

Rrrrrrr . . . ight. Rrrrrrr . . . ight.

'Really?'

Her warmth was comforting and he must have got to sleep eventually, for he had a terrible nightmare.

'Fire! Fire!'

Smelling the thatch burning, he leaped from the bed and ran for the door. He would have run outside if his father hadn't stopped him. Topheric held him close and soothed him.

'Look, look all is well. There is no fire.'

And when Topher was calm, Topheric said, 'Let us thank the God of the Cross and his mother for your dream, for it is a warning. Now I am sure that the scop was right. It is clear there is going to be an attack, but now at least we can prepare for it.'

It took Topher a long while to get back to sleep, even though Ka got back under the covers with him. He couldn't get the picture of a Viking attack out of his head. He saw the Danes leaping from their longboats with flaming torches. Hurling them onto the thatches of the Saxon houses. Raiding and ransacking as the Saxons fled. Killing those who didn't. Grabbing what they could before the buildings burnt to cinders. Piling livestock, textiles and metals into their boats, then leaving as quickly as they had come. Except that now they didn't leave, the scop had said. They stayed – as conquerors. He remembered the look in the scop's eyes as he sang, the careful way he spoke the words.

'Then ominous words came from Ingwar's big mouth,
"I've conquered the north, now I'm heading south."

Laugh if you wish, friends, but heed what I say,
Ingwar the Boneless is coming this way.'

'Topher, go to sleep.' Topheric's voice came out of the darkness. 'You have to be up early in the morning. But we will see the scop first, find out what he knows and warn the King.'

They got up early to call on Beric, whose living and sleeping houses were near the gate. It took Topheric several minutes to rouse him with shouts. When he did come out of his sleeping house, he was rubbing his eyes, catching his yellow hair in his long fingers.

'What can I do for you, Topheric?' He was his usual mild-mannered self.

'I need to speak to the scop,' said Topheric.

'A moment,' said Beric, letting the skin fall over the door as he went back inside.

But when he came back he was alone.

'Gone,' he said. 'He must have gone in the night. Now if you'll excuse me?' Yawning, he pulled back the door cover, and Sigeric came out – and Topher saw Beric put one of his long fingers over his lips.

Chapter 9

'Come,' said Sigeric, heading for the gate, where Cadgael and Alfmaer were now waiting. But Topheric held Topher back. When Aelfred and Aethelstan and then the rest of the boys' tithing joined the others, Cadgael called out, 'Come on, Topher! Remember what my father said. The crows will be at the corn!'

Aelfred and Aethelstan were getting into the skiff.

Topheric strode over to him with Topher in tow. 'Cadgael, where's your father?'

'Where your father?' Sigeric mocked his Danish way of speech.

But Cadgael cuffed him and said, 'My father is in his living hall, breaking his fast. Why isn't Topher coming with us?'

'Because he and I must both speak to your father. I will bring him later. Do not worry. He will do his share.'

But when they reached the hall, Haegel was alone there, and he did not seem worried by what they told him – the flight of the scop or Topher's dream. He had other concerns. Between bites of bread and gulps of ale, he asked, 'Why isn't Topher with the other boys? It does not go well with them if he does not pull his weight. As to his dream, well, I have heard he is a bit of dreamer, and not just at night.'

So Cadgael had told him about yesterday.

'My Lord—' To Topher's surprise, Topheric dropped to one knee before Haegel. 'You are a thane, I a mere carl, and from across the sea, but I beseech you. Listen to my words and call a meeting of the elders to see what they think.'

'Get up, Topheric. Get up.' Haegel stood up and shook his mane of fair hair. 'There is no need for that. I will call the elders, but I'm sure the scop would tell the King if he thought his story was true.'

'Quickly then,' said Topheric, who didn't seem to notice Haegel's bushy eyebrows rise. 'For while we wait a Viking attack comes closer.'

Haegel went to the door and Topher whispered, 'Father, try not to sound so chief-like.'

But Topheric didn't seem to hear. Sitting on the bench, he was drumming his fingers on the tabletop.

When at last all the elders were in the hall seated round the big table, Topheric told them of his concerns. Topher, standing before them on the floor below the dais, told them of his dream. They listened, most of them, carefully enough, but some shook their heads as he spoke. And when they spoke, each one in turn, they seemed more worried that Topher was not with his tithing. He must learn to pull his weight, one of them said and the others nodded. Everyone dreamed of house fires, said another. It was what they were all afraid of. But one elder, Wulfstan, an old man with only a few wisps of white hair, who didn't seem to be listening, suddenly said, 'Haegel, some of this rings true. Do you recall what I told you when I went to Thurston sheep fair

61

in the spring? There was talk then of a Danish leader – Ivarr or Ingvarr – something like that, from whom Good King Edmund bought peace, maybe a year ago. The King gave him two hundred horses, if I remember rightly, and the Dane gave his word never to attack East Engleland.'

'But what if he has broken his word?' said Topheric quickly, as the other elders sat back in their seats. 'We should tell the King what we have heard. Then he can summon the fyrd and be ready.'

'They did say that the Dane went north again, well pleased,' said Wulfstan.

'I bet,' said Topheric. 'But the scop said he is now moving south.'

'In a story,' said Haegel. He put his arm on Topheric's shoulder. 'Listen. King Edmund is a wise and holy man. He will have the measure of the man and he will have people keeping watch. The Danes have Northumbria and are satisfied. That's what I have heard. Why should they want more? Mercia is a buffer between them and us. King Aethelwulf and his son Alfred hold Wessex. We have the East. Let us all live side by side in harmony – like you and Gytha.' He added, 'You two have proved Viking and Saxon can live together in peace. You yourself have said that most Danes are traders not raiders.'

'But this Ingwar is not a trader. He is not trustworthy,' said Topheric. 'Even Danes do not trust him. As Wulfstan says, they call him The Fox for he is sly. He makes some think that his nature is as soft as his bones, but it is not true. He hides his true intent. Think of your Saxon riddles. Things are often not what they seem.'

He unpinned the bronze brooch holding his cloak and held it up so they could all see the face engraved on the metal.

'Your craftsmen know that appearances can deceive. Is that the face of a man or a monster?'

He turned it one way and then the other so they could see how the face changed from man to monster, depending on how you looked. But the elders didn't look at it. They shuffled in their seats and murmured to each other. Topheric was stepping over the mark that separated thane from carl, but he seemed unaware of their frowns.

'Topher dreamed that this village was burning,' he went on, and Haegel let his arm fall from his shoulder.

'Come, I am not so foolish that I have not taken steps to protect my people. We live in peace here, but we are ready for war. We have lookouts along the river from here to the coast. A Viking longboat would be spotted – and steps taken to deal with it – long before it reached our banks.'

'But what if they come by land?' Topheric shrugged off Wulfstan's restraining hand. 'What if Ingwar uses the horses we so generously gave him to return and attack? The Danes have changed. They have trouble in their homelands and they want ours. The time when they raided and left has long passed. Now they raid and stay. They may be close already. The scop said they were. Someone should go and tell King Edmund.'

63

But his point was not taken. Staneric, who had seemed so keen to fight while listening to the scop, said, 'Topheric, where would you be today if we treated all Danes as enemies?'

'At the bottom of the river, and I thank you, as I have every day since you fished me out of the water and gave me a safe place. You are good peace-loving people, too good I sometimes think, and I am now one of you. That is why I yearn to help you. Let me go and tell the King about Ingwar, who has war in his nature and in his name. There is still time. If King Edmund gathers enough men to form a fyrd larger than theirs, the Danes will not fight. I know their ways. They will not fight unless they can be sure of winning.'

But again Haegel shook his head. 'Topheric, we do not know where the King is. It is Haligmonath, remember? He is not in his hall at Berig. He has gone to some holy place to give thanks to God. It could be Ely or Medehamstede or some other abbey.'

'Then send someone, send several, to find him. Tell him he should be on his feet, or on the back of a horse, not his knees!'

'Enough!' Haegel spoke angrily. 'Carls do not tell thanes what to do. Thanes do not tell kings!'

But Topheric went on. 'The King should be gathering an army to be ready for Ingwar and his heathen horde. I beg you, let me go and look for the Danes. Let me find out if they are coming this way. If they are, I can find out what they are up to. As you know, I speak their tongue, I can find out where they are heading. I can discover their plans.'

'Spy on them, you mean?' Wulfstan looked towards Haegel, but he was on his feet. There was a clatter and scrape of benches as the other elders got to theirs. One of them said, 'We have talked too long. We need all the hands we can get in the fields or we will starve this winter. That is a greater danger. It is harvest time, and will be leaf fall before we know it. Topheric, you are needed in High Field.'

Another said, 'And you, Topher, join the other boys in Top Field. If you work hard you will sleep well.'

Haegel touched Topheric's shoulder. 'Come, and make sure you bank up the fires tonight and keep the water buckets full.'

But Topheric stayed seated, his face in his hands. What would he do now? Topher longed to ask him, but two of the elders hustled him away.

'Come,' said one of them. 'I'll row you to the other side of the river.'

For the rest of the day he couldn't forget his father's bowed figure and the dismay on his face when Haegel hadn't heeded his warning. What would Topheric do now, he wondered? His duty was to obey his thane, but he was a man of action. Would he do nothing when his family was in danger?

Chapter 10

Topheric didn't do nothing. Topher soon learned that when he reached the landing stage that evening. Folk gathered there stopped talking when they saw him getting out of the skiff. Something was wrong, that was obvious, and he hurried up the track ahead of Cadgael and Sigeric, to get home and find out what. When Beric called out, 'Topher, come here!' he pretended not to hear him.

But Cadgael caught him up and grabbed his arm. 'We obey our elders, remember?'

Beric was sitting by his reed racks. 'Ah, Topher. Sorry to be the bearer of bad tidings, lad, but you will know sooner or later, that your father has left the village.' He shook his head and Topher caught a rare glimpse of his eyes, still as a snake's. But his voice was soft. 'I feel heart-sore about it, as I could have stopped him. Please tell your mother, I did say, "Why aren't you in High Field, with the others?" But he walked straight past without a word. Just after noon, it was, carrying his fishing rod. Thought maybe he'd got the say-so from Haegel.'

Cadgael said, 'I'm sure you did your best, Beric.' But Sigeric started hopping from one foot to another. 'Topheric's gone a-Viking! Topheric's gone a-Viking!' Till his father clipped him round the ear.

*

Setting off home as quickly as he could – with Cadgael still close – Topher felt as if everyone was watching him. In the settlement most women were inside cooking the evening meal, but their men sat outside drinking ale and children were still playing on the grass. When they were nearly there, by Aethelstan's homestead, Cadgael said, 'Do you want me to come home with you?'

Topher shook his head.

'I'll be off then. God be with you.' Cadgael cut across to his father's hall and Topher broke into a run. Surely his mother would know where his father was? Jumping over the wicket fence, he headed straight for the living hall, and didn't see his grandmother till she spoke.

'Topher, it's good to see you.' Half hidden by one of the buttresses, she was bent over, shutting up the hens for the night, and must have heard his footfall. Grey-haired and sixty years old, her sight was failing, but she was a source of wonder to the rest of the village.

'Here, take this for your supper.' Straightening as far as she could, she handed him a warm brown egg. 'Give it to your mother. She's in the eating house. No, no, go on ahead,' she added when he waited for her. 'It will have hatched by the time I reach the fire.'

Eager to see his mother, Topher did what she bade, but when Gytha saw him, she put her finger to her lips. He gave her the egg and wondered why she hadn't hugged him in greeting. Instead she lowered the egg into the pot hanging over the fire. Then she went to fetch bread from the food store. His sisters weren't there, he noted. So they must be in the sleeping house already. Was that why his mother didn't want to talk? The girls would be out of bed as quick as ferrets if they heard him. Nor were his mother's brothers at home, though they usually ate as a family. The room seemed empty and even bigger than usual, and it always seemed big because there were no supporting posts inside, as in Saxon houses.

He learned later that his uncles were still searching for his father, with the rest of his tithing. But that was all he learned. His mother and grandmother didn't know where his father was. They hoped he would know something they didn't.

'Tell us everything you know,' said Grandmother when they gathered round the fire in the middle of the room. 'But keep your voice low, for walls have ears.'

He told them what had happened at the moot hall and they both nodded, for they knew already. Topheric had told them, and that the others had dismissed his fears, and spurned his advice.

'But it looks as if he has gone to look for the King anyway,' said Gytha.

'So why didn't he tell us?' said Grandmother.

'He must think that if he didn't, we cannot be blamed for not stopping him.'

His grandmother shook her head. 'But that is not how the tithing works. He knows that. We will be blamed for not knowing.'

And later, when his mother went to the sleeping house, to move Emric to her side of the bed, Grandmother said, 'And how are you, grandson? How does it fare in the boys' tithing?'

'It fares.'

'So what brought you home early, yesterday?'

So she had seen him.

'Ka,' he said shortly. 'Where is she, by the way?'

She hadn't come to greet him as she usually did.

'She's in the sleeping house, up in the rafters, where she fled when you brought her home yesterday. She has been there all day. Were the boys up to their old tricks?'

Part of him wanted to answer and Grandmother nodded as if he had. Sometimes it was as if she could see the thoughts in his head. 'What did they do to Ka?'

'They put her in the middle of a sheaf...'

When he'd finished she said, 'You must tell Haegel of this.'

'And make enemies of my whole tithing?'

'If Haegel found out he would punish you for *not* telling. We are Christians now, not pagans. If you do not tell, you will be punished along with those who did it. That is how the tithing works.'

'If I do tell I will be punished *by* those who did it.'

'You must do what is right, but maybe warn them first. Tell them you will go to Haegel if they act like that again. Try to get them to do right, but be wary. Watch Sigeric. He's a fool, and his father has the green-eye for your father. Now to bed, but say your prayers first.'

He whispered his prayers, kneeling before the wooden cross over the door. Then he turned to the statue in the middle of the sleeping house. Sigeric said it was Freya, the pagan goddess, whose chariot was pulled across the night sky by six grey cats. It wasn't. It was Mary, mother of the God of the Cross and he prayed to her too.

'Holy Mother, take good care of Mother and Father and Grandmother and Emric and Aemer and Ka, but especially Father.'

Where was Ka? He looked up and saw her green eyes shining out of the darkness. She jumped down from the rafters soon after. He felt her land on the bed near his feet and pad her way to the top. She nudged her forehead against his to greet him, before turning round and tunnelling under his woollen cover. Soon afterwards when she was sleeping in the curve of his stomach he heard Mother and Grandmother come to their beds, Mother to the double bed on the opposite side of the room where she usually lay with his father. Grandmother to a smaller bed in the corner where she lay alone beneath an old wolfskin even on summer nights. Her old bones ached, she said, but she got down on her knees to say her prayers.

'God bless Topheric and bring him safely back to us. Help Edwynn and Edmaer in their search.'

So Mother's brothers hadn't yet come back.

'God bless our children,' Grandmother went on, 'and keep them safe this night. Bring them sweet dreams ...'

Then Mother helped Grandmother to her feet and into bed.

Topher watched his mother pull the wolfskin over the old lady, and heard her say, 'Sweet dreams, Mother.' He heard Grandmother say, 'Sweet dreams, daughter.

Sweet dreams, one and all.' As if she knew Topher was listening.

But Topher's dreams weren't sweet. He dreamed again of a Viking attack.

Chapter 11

When he woke in the morning he was alone in the sleeping house. His sisters must have clambered over him to get out of bed. His mother's bedcover was hanging over the crossbeam, alongside his grandmother's wolfskin. The two women were up and about. He could hear their voices, in the living house next door, and other voices. Men's. His father's? He sat up to hear better. No, his mother's brothers. He recognised their angry tones. So they had returned and were having a row.

'Where has he gone? He must have told you!' That was Edwynn, Mother's younger brother.

'Shush, brother!' That was his mother. 'Walls have ears.'

'Don't shush me. There should be no secrets.'

'Least of all between brothers and sisters. Our strength lies in trust.' That was Edmaer, Mother's older brother. He spoke more gently. 'Sister, if you know where Topheric has gone, you must tell us. This secrecy is putting us all in danger. We are all at risk, saying we do not know where he has gone. What if they put us to the ordeal to see if we are lying?'

The ordeal! Surely that was used only when the moot could not make up its mind if someone was guilty, and had to leave God to decide. He had seen it done once when Alfmaer's uncle had been accused of stealing a sheep from his neighbour. He had had to walk barefoot on burning coals. Only when his feet healed quickly did the court believe that he was not guilty.

'I do not know where Topheric has gone!' Gytha sounded angry. 'How many more times do I have to tell you? All I know is that my husband is a good man. If Topheric said he was going fishing, he went fishing. If he has not come back it is through no fault of his own.'

'Then why did we find no sign of him or of Arrow at his fishing spot?'

Arrow went everywhere with Topheric. She was like his shadow.

'I – do – not – know.'

It went silent then.

Topher stroked Ka who had emerged from under the bedclothes. 'What do you think?' She seemed to be listening too.

'Do you think something has happened to him?'

Prrrraps. Prrrrraps.

'Then where is he?'

His mother was right. Topheric was a man of his word. If he'd said he was going fishing he'd have gone fishing. He often went fishing if he was in low spirits and usually came back feeling better, especially when he had caught a fish or a fat eel. Sometimes he needed to be on his own, he said. But he always told someone first, and he didn't go when he was needed to help. It was odd that Edmaer had found no sign of him or of Arrow. What if he hadn't gone fishing? Topher couldn't get the picture of his father, head in hands, out of his head. What if he had lied about where he was going? He might have committed one sin to prevent a greater. He had been so sure they were all in danger. Would he have sat around and done nothing? Would he have waited for the Vikings to attack? Of course not! Topheric was a man of action.

'Come on, Ka!'

Leaping out of bed, he ran to the living house in his shift, a vivid picture in his mind's eye – of his father returning with the King, side by side on horseback. Behind them was a huge fyrd, hundreds of fighting men, their spears gleaming in the sunlight. What had Topheric said? *The Danes will not attack unless they can be sure of winning. They respect a show of force.* And so when Ingwar saw King Edmund and a huge army he would not dare to attack. So, Topheric might have lied about where he was going.

His mother and her brothers were breaking their fast round the fire.

'You may be right,' said Edmaer, when Topher had had his say. 'But that still gives us three choices. He could have gone to find the King, or after the scop to find out more, or even to spy on the Danes. Either way, we don't know where to look. We can only hope he returns quickly.'

'He should have told us,' said Edwynn. 'We would have gone with him to see Haegel. We could have sent several men to look in different places.'

Grandmother handed Topher a bowl of oatmeal warmed by ewe's milk, but before he had time to eat it Sigeric appeared at the door. How long had he been listening?

'Cadgael sent me to get Topher. We've been waiting for him since cockcrow.'

Gytha grabbed Topher's cyrtle and pulled it over his head.

As his head emerged he saw Sigeric smirking. When they reached the boys on the riverbank, he said, 'Sorry it took me so long, lads. I had to wait for Topher's mother to dress him.'

For the rest of the day Topher had to put up with the other boys' jibes, but worse was to come when he returned in the evening.

Again, he could tell something was wrong as soon as he saw the crowd round the landing stage. He was in the first crossing, with Cadgael and Aethelstan and as Aelfred paddled the skiff over he felt everyone's eyes on him. But when he got out of the skiff, those same eyes looked at the ground – all except Beric's. He stepped forward and tried to take Topher's arm. 'Come on, lad. Your mother needs you.'

But Topher ducked out of his way, for he wanted no one near him.

Cadgael said, 'Have courage. I will come with you.'

But Topher ran up the slope followed by Beric who caught him up by the gate. Topher's shaking fingers fumbled with the catch.

Beric said, 'Let me do that, lad.' He opened the gate with one hand, and grasped Topher's arm with the other.

'No!' He tried to shake the man off. But Beric tightened his grip.

'Courage, boy. These things happen.' He steered Topher along the path. 'You are your mother's son, her eldest child and now you must be a man.'

Why? What things? He didn't ask, for he didn't want to know the answer.

Chapter 12

Arrow lay by the fire, but his white fur was red with blood. As Gytha dabbed at his wounds, the dog whimpered, and Emric and Aemer watched from behind splayed fingers. Grandmother stood by them. Ka, on the other side of the fire, was the first to notice Topher in the doorway. She raced to his side and rubbed round his legs. Then Grandmother saw him and held out her arms.

'W-what happened?' He let the words out.

Grandmother shook her head. 'We don't know. Arrow brought this home.'

She showed him Father's brooch, the one he'd shown to Haegel and the elders. But now, attached to the pin, were threads from his cloak. 'Perhaps a wolf or a bear attacked him.'

'No.' Gytha lifted her head. 'These wounds were made by man not beast. Look. These cuts were made by axes.'

Topher looked at the gashes in Arrow's side, though the sight made his stomach heave, as Gytha stroked the dog's head. 'They are straight, not jagged. Someone went at him as if he were chopping meat. But look,' she pointed to threads between Arrow's teeth. 'The animal put up a good fight.'

Silence. They were all thinking. Had Father put up a good fight? Was he lying wounded somewhere like

Arrow, but with no one to tend his wounds? Topher got on his knees to see the threads more clearly. Were they from his father's cloak or his attacker's? It was hard to say. They were blue and his father's cloak was blue, but so were many other men's. Father's cloak had a border of red and yellow and green, for he liked bright colours, and mother had woven a braid like a rainbow for him. But there was only blue and maybe red, between Arrow's teeth – and the red could be blood.

Grandmother broke the silence. 'I think Topheric was alive when Arrow left. He must have sent him home or the dog would have stayed by his side to the last.'

'Then we should be able to follow his track back to Father.' Topher felt hope rising.

'Track?' said a voice, and they all turned to see Beric in the doorway. 'There won't be any tracks. The ground is like iron. There hasn't been any rain for days.'

'Blood,' said Topher, feeling uncomfortable. He thought Beric had gone. 'I meant a trail of blood to Father, not paw prints in mud.'

And Grandmother nodded. 'Your uncles and the rest of your father's tithing thought of that and left soon after Arrow returned.' She walked over to Beric. 'I give you thanks for bringing Topher home, but we can manage now.' And as Beric left, dropping the skin over the door, Topher remembered what his grandmother had said about him.

'What did you mean when you said he had the green-eye for Father?' he asked.

'Oh.' Grandmother shook her head. 'Just that he feels hard done by, because your father is an elder and he isn't. But he has been kind enough today.'

At nightfall his uncles, Edmaer and Edwynn, came in stone-faced. Fair-haired and thickset, their cyrtles covered with dust, it was hard to tell them apart.

'W-where? What...?' said Gytha, when Topheric didn't follow them into the hall. Pulling at the long plait on her shoulder, she seemed afraid to speak.

'Be calm, sister.' Edmaer, the older brother, slightly taller, came and put his arms round her. Edwynn helped himself to water from a jug.

'Be strong. We did not find him, but we found where he last lay – or sat.'

'And ...?' Gytha prompted.

'He was not where he said he'd be. He was not at his usual fishing place, though we think he paused there. The others have gone to tell Haegel what we found.'

'What did you find?'

'Not much. There was no sign of a fight.'

'Then where did the blood come from?'

'Arrow, we know that.'

'But why would anyone attack his dog?'

'That we do not know, but we noticed that the grass was flat where he had been sitting on the bank, and where he had walked about. And where perhaps someone else had walked. Someone may have come up behind him. We cannot be sure. He was west of here, still north of the river. We think he sat on the bank to fish.'

'Then where was he heading if he was west of here?' Haegel's deep voice was unmistakeable. They all turned to see him coming through the doorway, his mane of hair just missing the rafters.

As Edwynn went to get him a seat, Haegel strode to the fire and crouched to fondle Arrow's ears.

'How is the animal? If only he could speak. But he can't, so others must.' He stood up and looked from one to the other sternly. 'Now, tell me everything you know, and what you think and why you let Topheric go off on his own. Then come to the moot hall in the morning and I will tell you what the elders and I have decided to do.'

He sat on the bench Edwynn offered and accepted a beaker of ale. The family all then spoke in turn and he seemed satisfied, Topher thought. He nodded a lot, even when Topher said he thought his father might have lied for the greater good.

But when he had gone Edwynn looked glum. 'He blames us, for we are Topheric's kin and of his tithing, and he is right. We should not have let this happen. He should have told us. Sister' – he put his face close to Gytha's – 'your husband should not have taken the law into his own hands. If you know anything ...'

Edmaer pushed him away. 'Brother, calm down. She does not know. She would tell us if she did.'

'I would,' said Gytha, fingering her amber beads, 'for I fear for his life.'

That night it took Topher a long time to get to sleep,

and when he did he had the dream again. He saw the settlement burning.

Next morning he went with his uncles to the moot hall. Haegel ruffled Topher's hair as he greeted them at the door. 'How's Arrow this morning?'

'Alive,' said Edmaer. 'Just.'

Was Topheric still alive? The question hung in the air, as they followed Haegel to the end of the hall where the other elders were already seated on the dais.

'What have you decided?' Edwynn voiced Topher's thoughts, even before Haegel was properly seated behind the table.

Edmaer elbowed his brother. 'Sorry, my Lord. My brother forgets his place.'

But Haegel looked sad rather than angry. 'You are not going to like this, I know, but we have thought long and hard and we have decided to wait.'

'Wait?' Topher couldn't believe it. 'What for?'

'Topher!' Now Edmaer elbowed him.

'As you know,' Haegel went on looking down at Topher, 'yesterday, when the trail was fresh, your uncles, in fact all your father's tithing, searched for your father. They were away many hours, and followed the trail for as far as it led.'

'To where Arrow was attacked,' said Topher, 'but only till dark. My father might still be nearby, lying injured. Or robbers may be holding him.'

'If they have, we will hear from them soon, asking for wergild.'

'But can't we seek them out and offer wergild?'

Haegel sighed heavily. 'Topher, your father acted alone without telling his tithing. He must accept what follows. We cannot spare men to go looking for him. We need all the men we have in the fields and cannot risk losing more.'

'But my father was trying to help us, all of us. He says we're in danger and must prepare for a Viking attack. I think so too. I think he was trying to get to the King, and I've had the dream again. Why don't you *believe*—?'

But Edmaer clamped a hand over his mouth.

For a moment he thought Edwynn might say something, but he shook his head as one of the elders said, 'Haegel, you are too forbearing. The boy should be whipped.'

Then both his uncles led him from the hall.

Edwynn said, 'I know how you feel, but Edmaer is right. You were making things worse. We don't want more trouble. It's best if you join your tithing in Top Field.'

Both uncles walked down to the river with him.

'There's my boat,' said Edmaer. 'I'll row you across to Top Field.'

Thoughts came into Topher's head. *I could row myself up river. I could go west where my father went. I could take Father's boat. Why didn't Father take his boat,* Sea Steed? *He'd have been faster in that.* More thoughts followed as Edmaer pulled on the oars. Where was his father's boat? He couldn't see it anywhere. But there was Beric in his usual place, plaiting rushes and watching everything.

Through the rest of the day he wondered how he could go and find his father, but there wasn't much time for thinking. He had to join in with the other boys' games, kick-ball and hide-and-seek, and a long game – it lasted all afternoon – of Saxons against Vikings. Cadgael put a circle of willow wands on his head and said he was King Edmund. Aethelstan said he was a Viking chief and they both chose sides. 'Topher,' said Cadgael, who chose first.

'Sigeric,' said Aethelstan.

They all made weapons by whittling sticks, and shields by bending hazel branches into circles with a holding bar across the middle. Then, standing close they formed two shield walls, and fought to the death, hacking at each other's legs, as they had been taught, jabbing above and below their shields. What would it be like fighting a real enemy, Topher wondered fleetingly, as he faced Sigeric? What if the Vikings really did come?

Chapter 13

'What are you plotting?' Grandmother was looking at him searchingly, and Topher's heart sank. How did she know he had a plan? He'd made some preparations too, not many for there wasn't time, but he had put a fish-hook in his pouch, for he would need to eat on the way.

'Nothing.'

They were alone, that was the only good thing, in the living hall, sitting by the fire. His mother had just gone to the sleeping house to make room for him in the children's bed. His uncles were outside making their sheep safe for the night. Someone had warned of a wolf on the prowl.

'It's no good trying to hide your thoughts.' Grand-mother shook her grey head. 'I can read your face. You are like your father in that way.'

'Then where did he go? Tell me that.'

'That much I couldn't read, but I think to look for the King, for he was heading west. For Ely Abbey, I think, and that is where you should go, with this.' She handed him a square of cloth. 'It's a gift to the Abbess there.'

'You want me to go?' That was a surprise. He studied the cloth which had strange marks on it. Runes, he knew that, for Grandmother had taught him to read his name, and yes, his name was there.

'You need not know what it says.' She took it from

him, rolled it up and picked up her needle. 'Just make sure the Abbess gets the message. And do not worry about what folk will say when they learn you have gone. I'll tell them I sent you, and blame my addled old brain for forgetting to ask leave.'

But what if they didn't believe her? Everyone knew Grandmother's brain was as sharp as her needle. And wasn't the family in enough trouble already?

'Quick, come here.' Swiftly she unpicked the hem of his cyrtle, and began to sew it up again, hiding the roll of cloth inside. 'Now listen carefully. Follow the river west, crossing it when you can. There will be a bridge or ferry for Ely is south of the river, an island in the middle of wetlands. You will see it easily, for its wooden tower is higher than anything else thereabouts. It sticks out of those wetlands like the mast of a ship. When you see it, find the causeway to Ely, which leads straight to it. You *must* find the causeway, mind, or you will surely drown. Look out for the quicksands. What looks like firm ground often isn't.'

She bit off the thread as Mother came in, and began to scold him. 'Just you be more careful in future. Look after your clothes. I don't want to be forever mending.'

Later, as soon as he was sure his mother and sisters were sleeping, he crept out of the sleeping house. Ka was sleeping too, in his bed with her tail over her face, and he left her there. The wetlands were no place for a cat. Grandmother, still awake, made the sign of the cross as he passed her bed. Earlier she'd crept in with bread and cheese, wrapped in a cloth and tied it to his belt. He would break his fast on that later. But first he must get out of the village without waking anyone.

The harvest moon bathed everything in a strange brown light. His shadow looked huge as it jumped along beside him. His shadow, he told himself, not a shadow walker. But it would soon be midnight when those spirits of the dead did walk the night. Trying not to think about them, or the wolf on the prowl, he thought instead of dangers closer to home, like the dogs that lay by the house doors. If they started to bark or howl he was done for. Best to walk boldly then, as if he had every right to be out at night, not creep like a thief. Straightening up, he saw Haegel's mastiff prick his ears and open an eye, as he passed their gate, but that was all it did. Staneric's hounds were more active as he reached the south side of the village. He froze as one of them, as big as a wolf, loped over, but all it did was sniff his legs with its cold wet nose. Off again, he headed for the east side, where there was a hole in the fence. That much he'd managed to find out earlier that day, and that the fence was too high to climb over. Here was another dog, but that too knew him, and like the others it was trained to stop strangers coming in, not villagers getting out. But what about geese? White shapes ahead, near where he thought the hole was, suddenly moved and started to honk!

Rigid, he went over what he'd planned to say if someone appeared. *I thought I'd left the gate open. I came out to check.* Pity he wasn't nearer the gate. But no one came, the geese went quiet, and there was the hole in the wattle. But too small to get through. Glad he'd brought his knife, he began to make it bigger, cutting through the branches as silently as he could, drawing them out as silently as he could. Then he climbed through, put some back, and then keeping close to the fence, followed it round till he came to the river.

At first he made good time, though he kept checking he wasn't being followed. But later, when the path curved away from the river, grass gave way to springy heather and he was slower. Lifting his feet high made his legs ache and sometimes a bird flew up in front of him like a small ghost. It seemed ages before he came to the next settlement, but when he did, all seemed quiet. He crept past and nothing stirred except the wind in the heather. Were the folk back in Haegellisdom still sleeping, he wondered? How long had he got before the rest of his family discovered he had gone? What would they do then? Tell Haegel straightaway? His uncles would want to, and it would be better for them if they did. But not for him, for Haegel would send someone to bring him back. Unless Grandmother could persuade him not to. What were the chances of that?

Moving as fast as he could, he saw the outline of another settlement ahead. When he reached it all was quiet, but he only had a few hours before people woke up. Work started in the fields as soon as the sun rose, and then someone would be sure to see a stranger passing by. He must keep going till there were several settlements between him and home. Just keep putting one foot in front of the other, he told himself. Left right, left right, left right – as lightly as he could so as not to leave tracks. But when he glanced behind, he saw a trail like a snail's. Flattened heather glistened in the moonlight. Hoping it would spring back as soon as the sun got up, he pressed on.

Now the path swung back to the riverbank and he made better time. The river glimmered in the moonlight. When he reached the next village it was still dark, but by the time he reached the next it was beginning to get light. There was smoke in the air, curling up from rooftops. People were stirring their fires. Skirting that village, he hurried on westwards. A cock crowed and now he could feel the sun on his back, and was that something moving in the field ahead? Yes, but man or beast he could not be sure. Soon though, he would meet someone, and then there would be questions. Another cock crowed and was answered by another. Rooks in the woods to the north started to clatter. More birds joined in. Soon the dawn chorus was deafening. What a racket. No one slept through that. Now his belly was rumbling. Could he stop to eat? He must go over his story too. He had to have a story. A boy travelling on his own would be asked questions. Good, there was a tree ahead, a willow with dangling branches.

It made a good hiding place. Leaning against its trunk, he ate some bread. Just a bit for it had to last. Later, he could make a rod and catch a fish, but now he must go over his story. *I am delivering a gift to the Abbess of Ely. It is from my grandmother.* It was Haligmonath when offerings were made to God, so people should believe him. What did it say on the cloth? Wishing he knew, he closed his eyes, and tried to see the runes in his mind's eye. Tried to read them, for he knew some of the signs. Yawned. How tired he was, for he had walked half the night. How good it would be to sleep. Perhaps a nap would do him good, make him go faster when he woke? He yawned again . . .

Then woke with a jolt. But kept his eyes tightly shut, for he was back in the sleeping house, he thought. Mother or Father was standing near. Any moment now one of them would tell him to get up, shake him when he didn't. Someone was very close. He sensed it.

'Ouch!' Something pricked his thigh. 'What the . . . ?'

Remembering the hidden weaving, he tensed. Someone was trying to steal it, must be picking at the stitches with a knife.

'S-top.' He forced himself to open his eyes, dreading whom he would see.

Chapter 14

No one. There was no one there.

He'd expected to see a man. Had been sure there was someone crouching at his feet, cutting through the cloth. But – he looked around – no one. No one at all. Fear had put pictures in his mind.

'Ouch!' Something pricked him again.

'Mwow!'

'Ka!' He almost cried with relief. 'I'm a simpleton!' Of course! He should have guessed. The weight of her was so familiar. She was on his thighs pull-pricking with her claws. Now she ran the length of his body and butted his forehead, growling.

Why did you leave me? Why did you leave me?

'I didn't think you'd want to come.'

She butted him again.

'It's a long way and it's going to be wet. You hate getting your feet wet.'

Prrrt! She butted him again and gave him her 'Don't be stupid' look, but when he stroked her back she began to purr.

'You've forgiven me?'

Rrrr. Rrrr. Insistently.

Rrrr. Rrrr. Meaningfully, but what did she mean?

Listening intently, he tried to cut out the sound of the wind in the heather and the yackety birds.

Hurrrrrrrry. Hurrrrrrrry. Hurrrrrrrrrrry.

'Is someone following me?'

Sigerrrrrrric. Sigerrrrrrrric. Sigerrrrrrrric.

'Oh no! Is he alone?'

Berrrrrrrric. Berrrrrric. Berrrrrric.

'He's with his father?'

Rrrrrright. Rrrrrrright. Rrrrrright.

'Why them?'

Trrrrrrrraitors.

'Traitors?'

Trrrrrraitors. She jumped off his chest, raced ahead, then stopped and looked back, her actions even clearer than her words. *Come on. There's no time to waste.*

'One moment.' He broke off a piece of cheese. 'Here, eat this.'

While she ate he wrapped up the rest and tied it to his belt.

Then they both set off at a brisk pace. How far was it to Ely? He scanned the horizon for a glimpse of the tower, sticking out like a ship's mast, but nothing, nothing at all jutted out of the flatness. Was it a day's walk? Three? He wished he had asked. And where and what was the crossing place? It could be a bridge or ferryboat, his grandmother had said. If only he'd had more time to talk to her. Wherever the crossing place was, there would be a settlement. There always was, but he couldn't see any sign of buildings.

It didn't rain; that was one good thing. Not seeing Beric or Sigeric was another. They saw hardly anyone, just the odd fowler or fisherman and they made it clear they didn't want to speak. They made good speed over the springy heather, and the cloudless dome of blue sky overhead promised more dry weather. Then, at around midday, the ground grew sandier, the heather sparser and eventually gave way to tussocks of tough grass. Were they nearing the wetlands?

That night, still on the heath, they slept under the stars. As he wrapped himself in his cloak and lay down in a sandy hollow, he hoped he was as well hidden as the birds he'd nearly trodden on that day. Startled, they'd flown into the air and Ka had sometimes caught one. In one nest he'd found a clutch of eggs, which though raw, had made a welcome meal. There wasn't time to build a fire and it was too risky, as grass and heather were tinder dry. Now, as he prayed to the God of the Cross to help them, Ka nestled in the curl of his stomach. It was good to have her there.

But she woke him early next morning, licking his face with her rough tongue.

Hurrrrrrrry. Hurrrrrrrrry.

It was noon when they saw the bridge. At last! There was a settlement too, as he'd expected. Longing for a proper meal he said, 'Let's go!' and broke into a run. Surely they were far enough away from Haegellisdom now?

But Ka hung back, urging caution. *Carrrrrrrrreful. Carrrrrrrreful.*

'You're right of course.'

When they reached an oak tree further up the riverbank, she scrambled up its trunk. He climbed it too and got a good view of the village straddling the river. Like Haegellisdom, perhaps a bit bigger, there were a lot of people about. Some were in the fields, others on the river and even more on the bank, loading and unloading boats. Well, that's what he thought. He couldn't be sure. Was Ka's eyesight better than his? Smoke rose from the thatched rooftops and he thought he could smell meat cooking.

'Aren't you hungry, Ka?'

Ssssss. Rrrrrrrrr.

Ssssss. Rrrrrrrrr.

At first he thought she was hissing and growling. It took him a few moments to realise she was saying, 'Sssstay herrrre!'

Then she was off, down the tree and over the heather.

Hidden in the tree, he watched her make her way to the settlement. When he couldn't see her any longer, he stayed in the tree, till hunger made him come down and search for food. Ka had said 'Stay here.' Well, he wouldn't go far, and he would keep a good lookout, but he needed to eat. He found some blackberries, but they didn't fill him, so he dug for worms, made a rod from a branch and a piece of string and the hook he had with him, and headed for the riverbank.

And it was there in the water, that he saw the body. At first he wasn't sure it was a body. Perhaps it was a log. There was scum round it and other flotsam – leaves and sticks and a dead crow. They all looked as if they had been there for some time. The water round them looked oily. Then he saw a hand, a puffy hand floating on the surface. It *was* a body, in the water, face down. For a while he just stared. A dead body. He had seen dead bodies before. He had been to funerals and looked into coffins before the lid was nailed on, and that wasn't scary at all. It was showing respect. But this was scary. He didn't want to look at it. But then he noted a strand of hair floating on the surface, reddish brown hair, and his heart stopped. Forcing himself to move forward, he crouched down and lifted the head, which seemed stuck face down in the mud, it was so heavy. Then – schluck! – it came out at last, but he couldn't see the face. Still not sure, he lifted it higher, till bending low he could see underneath. Just. And he let it go, belly heaving and eyes brimming. As the head hit the water, the little he'd eaten in the last two days spilled onto the grass.

It was mid-afternoon when Ka returned and found him still on the riverbank. The body was still in the river. He hadn't been able to move it. All he could do was cover it with leafy branches and weep. Heart-sore, he wept till there were no more tears inside him. He wept for all the things that would never happen again. He would never see his father's hair shining like copper. Never feel his sturdy legs supporting his back as he listened to a scop. Never feel his strong arms lifting him onto his shoulders. Never listen to his stories about polar bears and walruses and the snowy lands in the north he'd sailed to in his youth.

Prrtt. Prrt. You should be hiding. Ka was cross, for at first she didn't see the body.

Then he nodded towards the water and she went to see it. Returning, she was silent for a moment, her head bowed. But then she climbed onto his lap and began to lick his face with her rough tongue.

So . . . rry. So . . . rry. So . . . rrry. She purred like a hive of bees.

But when he began to weep again, her purrs became urgent.

Prrrt. Prrrt. Come on now. Move. There's no time to waste.

But he couldn't move. Couldn't stop weeping, couldn't stop remembering, couldn't stop dreading what was to come.

Rrrrrr. Rrrrrr. Get up. Move.

'Ouch!' She'd bitten his hand, none too gently, growling, *Berrr-ic. Berrr-ic.*

'Beric! Where?'

He . . . rrrrre. He . . . rrrrre.

'Here?'

Sigerrrrrrrrrric. Sigerrrrrrrrrric.

'Him too?'

'*Rrrrrrrrriver. Rrrrrrriver.*'

Ka must have seen them both at the crossing. Now they must be waiting there for him. Watching. Asking everyone they met if they had seen a boy passing through. They knew he had to cross the river to get on the causeway leading to Ely.

'You're right, Ka. We must find another way.' Wiping

his eyes on his cyrtle, he got to his feet.

It was hard leaving his father, who should have been buried with honour. But now he, Topher, must try and do what Topheric had tried to do – warn the King and save East Engleland.

Chapter 15

Hoping there was another bridge further up, they set off again, backtracking for a bit to get clear of the settlement. Then they went north round the east side of the higher land on which it was built, avoiding people working in the fields. When they were on the north side, they headed west again. On higher ground now, they could see the river below them, but they couldn't see any more bridges. Nor could they see any fishermen as the banks became less distinct. Were they getting close to the fens? It seemed as if they were. The air was salty now. Topher could taste it on his lips and he could hear the wind whipping across the wetlands. If only he could see a fisherman with a skiff, for they must cross the river before nightfall. The wetlands were full of dangers, trolls with huge mouths that sucked you under the mud, bog people with scaly skin and flipper hands and sinking sands that looked like solid ground. With wide-open eyes he scanned the landscape, but saw no one, no one at all, and soon the sky ahead was streaked with crimson.

Night was coming, but they trudged on till the land changed, dropping abruptly and sandy heath gave way to a grassy plain. For a while the ground felt firm and smooth and they went faster. Then it seemed to give under his feet.

Then Ka refused to go further. 'Mwow!'

He stepped forward and his foot sank into mud. When he tried to pull it out, the mud sucked at his shoe. Stepping back onto firmer ground, he had to leave it there, then lay full length on the grass and try to dig it out. And Ka watched with an 'I told you so' look on her face, till shoe in hand at last, he moved further back.

'If you know so much, tell me how we're going to cross that!'

Acres of swamp lay before them, and beyond that a gleaming expanse of water, shimmering red and gold, dotted by islands where grasses waved. The river ran into what looked like an inland sea, though it was impossible to tell where water ended and sky began. Then he saw something black on the red and gold, several things, a line of things moving across the landscape from right to left. At first they looked like black dots, but as he watched the dots lengthened, and he thought they might be wading birds.

'What do you think, Ka?'

She didn't answer, just watched intently, and so did he, and gradually, the shapes became bigger and clearer for they were getting nearer. Not birds, but men of some kind, he eventually realised. Lots of them were moving across the shimmering surface. But mortal men couldn't walk on water or mud, so what were these creatures? Bog people? Trolls? They still weren't close enough for him to see their clothes or features, only their long black shapes. But the shapes got longer as he watched. How, *how* were they moving in a straight line like that?

Because there was a causeway beneath their feet! Of course! What a fool he was not to think of that earlier. It must come from a settlement to the north, and most probably led to the one he needed to be on. So how could he get onto it, and who were these people? More of them were coming over the horizon, and not just men, horses too, lots of horses. *Heathen horde*. As the words came to his lips he pressed himself full length against the ground.

Had they seen him? They didn't have the sun in their eyes, so if they were looking sideways they could have easily. Hoping they hadn't, he began to wriggle backwards towards the heath. Ka, faster, reached it before him. When he caught her up they lay side by side on their bellies, watching the shapes becoming clearer – till suddenly Topher gasped with relief and joy as he recognised the long habits and black cowls of holy men. The leader, now only a hundred paces away, held a silver cross which glinted in the setting sun. It was a holy procession. These were monks not Vikings, pilgrims not plunderers on their way to Ely! So he could go with them if he could find a path to the causeway!

Wait! The word was in his mouth, when Ka clawed his hand.

'*Sssssssstop!*' she hissed.

'Why?' But he stayed silent and she withdrew her claws.

Now came more men in everyday dress. Long-haired men in britches, cyrtles and cloaks trudged steadily forward. Some had spears. Others had bows over their shoulders. Some had round shields. Then came more monks, one on horseback. A boulder of a man; he towered above those who walked with him, two in front of the horse, two behind. And behind them were more men in everyday dress, and more horses, and then more men for as far as he could see. The procession seemed to move silently, for the sighing wind drowned all other sounds. But as the sun dropped behind the horizon, the wind dropped too and they could hear the steady clop of horses, the rhythmic creak of the causeway and voices, one so high-pitched he thought at first it was the mewing of a curlew. Then, when it brought forth a guffaw from the guards, he realised it came from the fat monk. He said, he *squeaked*, something else – Topher didn't catch what – but the men laughed again, till suddenly the huge man lurched sideways and the monks with him sprang to his side to hold him on his mount. And now the folk behind crashed into him and one just behind fell right off the causeway into the mud. Only then did a shout go up to everyone else – and Topher recognised the Danish word for 'Stop!'

Chapter 16

'Stop . . . stop . . . stop!'

Like an echo the word went down the line, as more men moved forward to try and haul the huge monk back onto his horse.

'Stop! Stop! . . . op!'

The cry became fainter and fainter and gradually the line came to a standstill. Except for the men trying to haul the huge man back onto his horse, and others reaching out to the man floundering in the mud. While the line was still Topher tried to count them. At fifty he gave up for the light was fading, and there were many more than fifty. The line stretched into the distance. He had never seen so many men at one time, even when the whole village was gathered in the moot hall. There must be hundreds of men and hundreds of horses too. *Hordes. Heathen horde.* The words were on his lips again. These were Danes. There was no doubt about it. He'd learned some Danish from his father. The huge monk was a Dane.

When they moved off again it was nearly dark. Topher lay watching till the last one was out of sight. Then he lay listening to the creaking causeway and saw them only in his mind's eye. Were they going to travel right through the night? When at last the creaking stopped a rushing sound filled his ears and he tasted salt again. Was it the wind or the tide? Folk said it rushed in from the place they called Wash, because it washed over the land, flooding all but the highest bits. So did it come this far? Were he and Ka in danger here? So what should they do? Go back and risk meeting Beric? Could they cross the bridge without being seen in the dark? Could they find the bridge? It was very dark for the wind had brought in clouds. There was no moon or stars. Ka settled on his lap, her round eyes the only light in the darkness, but sleep wouldn't come. There were too many questions in his mind and he was sad, hungry and frightened.

He was sure he had seen the Viking leader, disguised as a monk. He was sure he had seen the Great Heathen Horde, heading for Ely Abbey. They must have sacked one abbey already, to get the monks' habits and the jewels and silver. He remembered the holy cross. When they reached Ely they would kill the nuns and do the same again. Kill the King too, if he was there. Then take over the country. But not if he, Topher, got there first and warned the King! But how? How could he cross the swamp and reach Ely before they did? He wasn't even sure where Ely was. So far he'd seen no sign of the abbey.

Ka began to purr. *Rrrr ...st. Rrr ...est.*

How could he rest? There was no time to waste. He should be on the move, finding a way across the swamp.

Rrrrr ...est. Rrrr ...est.

She was right. It would be best to rest till it was light, then find a way to the causeway, and somehow get to Ely before the Danes. Warn the Abbess. Give her grandmother's message. Urge the King, if he was there, to summon the shire fyrd and stop the Danes in their tracks and . . .

Rrrr . . . est. Rrrr . . . est.

Now Ka settled in the curl of his belly, like the hot stone his mother wrapped in a cloth if he had an ache. Trying not to think about his mother because that made him remember his father, he felt his eyelids grow heavy. Then he must have napped because when he opened his eyes, he felt cold and wet and dawn was breaking.

It was raining, or the wind was wet with spray from the sea. Behind them in the east the sky was streaked with gold. Ka stirred. Sheltered by his body she wasn't wet, but when she felt the rain on her whiskers, she looked at him accusingly.

'It's not my fault.'

They both looked out over the flat grey-brown landscape, and Topher remembered the thoughts he'd had before he slept. *Find a way to the causeway, catch up with the Danes and somehow skirt round their camp and get to Ely before them.* But now he wasn't sure he could see the causeway. That might be it maybe a hundred paces away, but there was no obvious path to it. He remembered his grandmother's warning about sinking sands. If he tried to walk he might drown.

'How are we going to reach that, Ka?'

She was staring at something. He followed her gaze and saw a face in the mist.

At first glance he thought it was Sigeric and froze. Then he thought it was a troll for its mouth was wide.

Then he thought it was a frog, though it was boy-sized and the colour of mud. It was crouching only ten paces away, its knees level with its chin. Was it one of the bog people he'd heard about? Folk said they could move over the fens like frogs, for they seemed to know where to put their feet without sinking. *So he could show me how to get to the causeway!* As the thought formed, he cupped his hands and called out, 'Hail! I am a friend.'

And the boy was off like a frog, leaping from sod to sod, gliding over the grass.

'Wait!'

But the boy didn't wait. He kept leaping from one sod to another, now in one direction, now in another, zigzagging for perhaps two hundred paces. Then he stopped – on the causeway, Topher thought – for then he ran in a straight line before vanishing into the mist.

'Did you see that, Ka? There *is* a safe way to the causeway.'

She had seen. She'd been watching intently.

'Can we do what he did?'

She moved first, jumping over the heather till she came to the edge of the heath. Then she surveyed the fen, moving her head from side to side. When he caught up with her he tried to recall where the boy had put his feet. The rain had stopped, but he could see nothing as definite as a path. There was, maybe, a zigzag line of flattened grass between them and the causeway. He couldn't be sure, so he felt for the stone he kept in the pocket on his belt. Threw it where he thought the track was. Saw it drop and sink.

'What do you think, Ka?'

She set off to the right, and he followed for twenty paces. Then, after a few moments of peering intently, she stepped onto the fen. It bore her weight, but would it bear his? Ka was light and light-footed and moved fast. She ran to where the boy had crouched, he thought.

Mia-OW! She'd stopped on a tussock. *Come on!*

Had the bog-boy walked on that bit?

Mia-OW! Come on!

He stepped down and the ground moved. It was like stepping onto a boat, but his foot stayed dry.

Prrt. Quickly!

She was right, the quicker the better. He made his way towards her and she started to leap, first this way, then that, but getting closer to the causeway all the time, following the frog boy's track, he thought. And he followed her, quickly, lightly, almost flying.

Ka was already on the causeway.

Each step brought him nearer to her, though sometimes it seemed to take him away. But at last he could see it, one leap away.

Prrt! Come on!

It lurched as he landed, and he swayed from side to side. It felt none too safe, was only wattle hurdles and cowhides, strung between sunken tree-trunks. How had it held all those men and horses? When he'd steadied himself, he peered into the mist along its length, but couldn't see anyone. It seemed odd that so many could disappear so fast. Had they walked though the night or were they sleeping? Crouching down, he looked for the humps and lumps of sleeping or sitting bodies, but horse droppings on the causeway were the only sign that they had passed that way.

Prrt! Come on! Ka set off.

He felt like a giant as he strode forward, as if people for miles around could see him. Crawling would be safer, but far too slow so he pressed ahead, hoping the sea mist was hiding him from any watching Vikings. He must catch up with them. Must get past them. Must get to Ely before them.

After a while a watery sun broke through the cloud, on his left. What did that mean? That he was travelling south, but he needed to go west. The sun wasn't good news either. As it got lighter and the mist cleared, people up ahead would be able to see him. But he still couldn't see the Danes. Where had they gone? And where was Ely? There was still no sign of the abbey. All he could see was flatness. Had the Danes burned it down already? Hoping the first sign of Ely wouldn't be smoke and flames, he pushed on. He had no choice, but gradually his footsteps got slower for he was tired and hungry. Was there anything to eat growing by the side of the causeway? He stopped to look, saw some sorrel leaves and heard Ka.

Mia-OW!

She had stopped too, but further up.

Mia-OW!

Grabbing some leaves, he caught her up, and saw they had come to the end of the causeway.

Chapter 17

But luck was with them at last. There was another causeway joining it. Going from east to west, it must be the one they should have got onto at the bridge. And there was Ely in the west, rising out of the mist like a ship at sea, the abbey's square tower like a mast. Topher pointed to fresh horse droppings on the causeway to their right.

'That way, Ka. West.'

Ca...rrr...efully.

'Of course.'

The Danes had moved fast. They must have travelled through most of the night. So where were they now? As the mist cleared Topher could see other buildings clustered round the abbey. It seemed to be in the middle of a settlement. Were the Vikings there already? If so they were probably sleeping, but what about the people who lived there. Did they know the Vikings were there too? Were they asleep in their beds? It was early morning after all. From afar all looked quiet. As they got closer they could smell wood smoke and horses, hear the occasional whinny. The smell of horses grew stronger the closer they got, and soon they could see them, lots of horses in the fields surrounding a cluster of thatched buildings. Ely looked a lot like Haegellisdom except for the abbey, but there was no fence round it. Instead there was water. Ely was an island, he remembered, as he saw two men at the end of the causeway.

Hoping they hadn't seen him, he lay flat and then wriggled forward. Ka ran along beneath him, on the marshy ground below the causeway, till it gave way to water. Then she joined him on the causeway, keeping close. Vikings. He was sure the men were Vikings. They were tall and Danes were nearly always taller than Saxons. But it was their voices that made Topher even more certain. Their slurred whispers carried across the water. Ingwar and his heathen horde were definitely here. Now able to see their long fair hair, braided in the Danish way, Topher flattened himself against the hurdles and waited. What should he do now?

The abbey, where he wanted to be, seemed further off. He could still see the top of its tower behind the other buildings, but it was a long way behind. In fact it didn't look as if it was part of the village at all. If it were not, how would he get to it? The isle of Ely, that's what people said. Now it looked as if the settlement ahead was a separate island. Movement in the village broke into his thoughts. The men at the end of the causeway were still there, were still staring straight ahead. But there were men behind them moving about. Lots of men were creeping around the other buildings. One had a flaring torch and suddenly hurled it. For a moment nothing happened. The flames seemed to die. Then a thatch flickered. Further along it straw flared. Soon flames were dancing along the rooftop.

'F...ire!' The word died on lips as Ka's fur filled his mouth. She was pressing her side against his lips.

Sssh. Ssssh. Look.

Sick with shame, he kept quiet, for the men at the gate seemed to be looking straight at him. What good would it do to shout? The people in the building wouldn't hear him, but the guards would.

He had seen buildings burn before. Often a spark from a hearth fire set light to a thatched roof in the settlement. But as soon as someone gave the alarm, folk would rush out to safety, and others would try to smother the flames or douse them with water. But now, though the flames were spreading, no one gave the alarm. It was strangely quiet. No one rushed out. No one shouted even when flames leaped into the air and raced along the thatch. Smoke billowed. Showers of sparks burst into the sky. Then a man appeared in the doorway. And a Viking knocked him to the ground. A woman came to the door and she was knocked down too. Men, women and children now tried to get out of the burning building, and fell to the ground as Vikings felled them with swords and spears and cudgels. Soon there was a pile of bodies blocking the door. Someone inside screamed. Then, as the roof collapsed, people appeared in the doorways of other buildings, but Vikings barred their exit.

'Have a good look!' he heard one of them say. 'Then get back inside, Saxon scum. And keep quiet or the same will happen to you!'

Topher crept away, back along the causeway, till he thought they couldn't be seen.

'What shall we do, Ka?' He felt full of shame, for he'd watched a hall burning and done nothing.

She rubbed against his face.

Warrrn. Warrrrrrrrn.

'Warn the nuns?' Didn't they know already? Surely someone from the abbey must have seen the fire.

Warrrrn. Warrrrrrn. Ka was insistent.

Tired and thirsty, Topher cupped his hands and scooped up some water from beside the causeway. He remembered the message for the Abbess sewn into his cyrtle. If the nuns saw the fire they might have thought it an accident. House fires often broke out. Or they might not have seen it. The abbey was further away than he thought. And it had been strangely quiet. He hadn't heard any Viking shouts and only one Saxon scream. The Vikings had been crafty. They hadn't celebrated afterwards with their singing and dancing. They'd burned one building only and kept quiet while they were doing it. Why? Because they didn't want the nuns to know they were there.

Warrrn. Warrrrn.

'You think we should go to Ely? But how?' They couldn't go through the settlement.

Trrrrrrrry. Trrrrrrrry.

Ka rubbed against his arms – but suddenly stopped. He felt her stiffen, saw her fur bristle. Saw her tail lashing from side to side. She was looking back down the causeway from where they had come. Turning to see what she was looking at, he couldn't see at first, because the sun was in his eyes. Then he saw two dark shapes coming towards them, one tall and slightly stooped, one half his size, and his heart stopped beating.

110

Chapter 18

They were coming this way. There was no doubt of that. But there was no escape, no point in running. They had seen him – he could tell – and he knew who they were. He knew that eager gait. The taller figure was usually bowed over a basket.

Ka growled, her fur like a brush.

But all he could do was wait. 'What can we do? Run back to the Vikings?'

He felt the causeway shaking or was he shaking?

The figures walked jauntily, seemed to bounce.

Later, he wished he'd slipped into the water and hidden under the causeway. He could have cut a reed and used it as a breathing tube. He could have tried to swim. So why hadn't he? Because he felt doomed? Because he felt that the Wyrd, the three grey sisters who sit at the foot of the tree of life spinning fates, had already spun his? But that wasn't true, he told himself. It was pagan nonsense. Every man was in charge of his own fate. That's what Christians believed. So he must keep his wits about him.

'Topher! Haegel sent us to bring you back home!' Beric grasped Topher's shoulders. 'I have good news. Your father has returned!'

Liar! But Topher didn't say that. Nor did he remove Beric's hands, though they made him feel sick. Better to tell Beric as little as possible.

Sigeric smirked.

'Let us return then.' Topher was surprised to hear his own voice so steady.

'When we have broken our fast.' Beric nodded at the settlement ahead. 'Let's see what we can find there. I think it is called Swindune.'

'I would rather go home.'

'Later.' Beric laughed and tightened his grip, and turned Topher towards the village.

Why did he bother to pretend?

Sigeric didn't. He pranced at their side. 'We're going to see the Vikings! We're going to see the Vikings!'

Till Beric cuffed him round the ear.

The guards at the gate, both a head taller than Beric, stopped them. 'What do you want, Saxon scum?' They spoke in Danish. Topher pretended he didn't understand. Beric got the drift and felt for something under his cloak, a bone hanging from his belt. He showed it to them. Clearly it was a sign. Were there marks on it? Topher guessed there were for the guards let them pass. At first they didn't see any more Vikings, only their horses, and when they reached the burned-down hall, the bodies of Saxons lying where they had fallen.

Beric laughed. 'Our friends must all be sleeping off their ale.'

But Sigeric was silent and looked pale. Was this the first time he had seen the handiwork of his father's friends? They stepped over the bodies of a man and woman and three children. Other dwellings seemed unharmed. Were people cowering inside them? A crow flew down and started to peck at the lip of a little boy.

Then a dog barked and a Viking appeared in a doorway of a building just ahead. He had hair tied back like a horse's tail and called out, 'What do you want?'

Beric stepped forward, showed him the bone and said, 'Ingwar!' very loudly.

The man said, 'Wait.'

Beric beckoned for Sigeric and Topher to join him. He was standing by a dead body, a man whose throat had been cut. Flies buzzed round his throat. The horse-tailed Viking came out with another man, bald as an egg, except for wisps of red hair round his ears.

This man looked at them and said, 'Sit there.' He pointed to the ground by the door and went back inside with Horse Tail.

Beric said the bald man was Ingwar's steward, so he must have met him before. When? Topher wondered. How long had he been a traitor? Now the three of them sat down with their backs against the wall of the building. It was nearly as big as the hall that had burned down. Sigeric moved away from the dead body.

Beric laughed, 'You'd better get used to it.'

Topher, though scared and hungry, watched as much as he could – and he kept a lookout for Ka. She had disappeared soon after Beric and Sigeric had turned up. Where was she now? It was a good place to see what was going on. They were on a thoroughfare and he could see several buildings. When men, Vikings not Saxons,

113

started to emerge from doorways, he tried to work out how many there must be. A hundred at least, he thought, and about fifty horses. So where were all the others? He was sure he'd seen more.

He listened hard. He looked like a Saxon, and so did Beric and Sigeric, so the Danes passing by talked freely, thinking they couldn't understand. Restless and eager for action, they were being made to wait – that was clear. Ingwar was waiting for two of his brothers – Hvitserk and Bjorn – and another leader from across the sea, a man called Guthrum, before he would attack. He was going to attack, but only when the Danes outnumbered the Saxons fivefold. A huge army was gathering in the woods at Thetford, to the east. Meanwhile Ingwar was lying low. He didn't want the nuns in Ely to know his army was there – yet. They would send for help from Wessex or Mercia if they knew. Also he wanted to be sure that the King was there before he attacked.

'So why doesn't he let us go and find out?' said one of the Danes.

They talked about the treasure in the abbey, the gold and silver and jewels. From time to time one of them went down to the river to see if any longboats had been seen. Bjorn and Hvitsek were coming by river from the Wash.

Topher remembered what his father had told him. The Danes hated losing men, because they could not replace them quickly. They had to wait for more shiploads from across the sea. They only fought when they were sure of winning without losing a lot of men. But now hundreds of fresh fighting men were about to arrive. The Danes were planning an attack on many fronts. They were intent on conquering East Engleland.

'What is it?' Beric was watching him. 'What are they saying?'

'I don't know.'

'Liar,' said Beric.

Then Topher saw Ka. She was on the roof of the building opposite, lying low with her belly close to the thatch. Their eyes met. But then she turned as if she'd heard something. A mouse he guessed. He saw her rear wiggling. She sprang. Yes, a mouse. Now it dangled from her mouth.

'Looks like that cat of yours.' Beric had seen her too. 'Bet that's the bakehouse.'

The smell of baking bread drifted across. Smoke filtered out through the thatch. Ka played with the mouse, dropping it, then catching it again. Suddenly Topher had an idea. Without looking down he felt for the hem of his cyrtle.

'Bet there's a woman there, baking,' said Beric.

Ka climbed to the ridge of the roof, with the mouse in her mouth, then disappeared down the other side.

Topher began to pick and pull at the thread holding his hem.

Beric stood up. 'I'm hungry. Stay here.' He strode to the bakehouse.

The steward appeared soon after. 'Where's the Saxon?'

Topher remembered to look as if he didn't understand, till the man shouted and pointed to where Beric had sat. Then Topher pointed to where Beric had gone and the steward went after him.

'What are you doing that for?' Sigeric inched closer.

'What?'

'Picking at your cyrtle.'

'I am?' He tried to jest. 'I am unpicking the thread of my fate.'

Sigeric didn't laugh. Well, it wasn't much of a jest.

Topher stopped picking for a bit and saw Ka on his right side. She was peeping round the corner of the building they were leaning against. Hoping Sigeric hadn't seen her too, he got to his feet, said he was going to pee, and went after her.

Ka was finishing the remains of a mouse.

Topher pulled the rolled-up weaving from his hem and bound some of the unpicked thread round it. Then he dangled it in front of her and looked into her eyes.

'Take this to the Abbess.'

She batted it with a paw. It did look a bit like a mouse.

'In the abbey.'

She didn't do anything and for a few moments he wished she were a dog. She was a clever cat, much cleverer than most, but he had never asked her to do anything like this before.

'Do you understand?'

She didn't answer, but took it from his fingers with her mouth.

'What are you up to, boy?' Beric, his mouth full of bread, was coming back from the bakehouse. The steward was with him.

Ka slid off, with the little bundle dangling.

Beric took hold of Topher's arm. 'We must go. The Viking leader is ready.'

The steward led the way to the door of the hall. Guards on either side demanded their weapons. Beric handed over his spear and short sword. Topher and Sigeric took their knives from their belts.

The steward hissed, 'Keep your eyes down. Do not look at Ingwar if you wish to live.' Then he lifted the pelt over the doorway and they followed him into the dark hall.

Chapter 19

It was hard to see, especially with eyes cast down. But as his eyes got used to the gloom, Topher could make out the leather boots and hide britches of men at the sides of the room. There were a few women too. He saw the patterned hem of a long blue dress as he passed the fire in the middle of the hall. Torches on the walls cast more light. There were more of these at the far end, where they were heading. But when the guards stopped, though it was lighter than the rest of the room, Topher was standing in shadow. Sensing someone looming over him, he guessed they were in front of the Viking chief. Risking a glance, he saw a dais and a table with men's boots beneath it.

'Who is this? And why have you brought him here?'

The squeaky voice made Topher look up, then down very quickly. He caught a glimpse of wild black hair and a bushy beard with a red hole in the middle. Had the squeak come from that? Ingwar, for this was surely he, reached the roof beam, though he was seated. Guards standing behind him looked small. Their long-shafted war axes looked like birds on the Viking leader's shoulders.

As the steward translated his words for Beric, Topher sneaked another look, first at Ingwar's neck, held upright by a wide gold brace, then his arms, thick with bangles.

He heard Beric say, 'It is Topher, son of Topheric, a Dane turned Saxon, Lord,' as words came into his head. *Arms so strong they could kill with one stroke.*

'A traitor, where is he?' Ingwar squeaked.

'In the river, my Lord.'

'In the river?'

'I put him there, my Lord.' Beric sounded proud. 'To stop him warning the King.'

'So he knew where the King was?' Ingwar's voice went higher.

'He hoped he was at Ely, my Lord.'

'So do we all.'

The men round the table laughed.

'And his chit,' said Ingwar. 'What has he done?'

'He was on his way to warn the King,' said Beric.

'Well, Saxon chit, look!' Ingwar pointed to a man hanging from a beam, upside down. 'See what happens to Saxons who cross me!'

As the man flinched – for a guard held a torch against his cheek – Topher recognised the scop. Laughing, Ingwar turned back to the men at the table, his jarls, who all seemed keen to have their say.

Most wanted to sack the abbey that day. 'Why wait?' one asked. The warriors were restless and raring to go. They would start fighting among themselves, said another, if they couldn't get at the Saxons. But Ingwar overruled them.

'An hour or so will make them keener. I'll feast them tonight and that will keep them happy. Meanwhile, you' – he pointed to Beric – 'can pop over to Ely and assure

119

the ladies that all's well in Swindune, and *find out if the Saxon King is there.'* He touched a bangle on his arm. 'This is yours when you come back with proof. For when we burn the abbey, we want to be sure we're burning King Edmund too. I want to show the Saxons his charred carcass, for when they see it they'll fall to their knees and the fighting spirit will leave them.'

When the steward had translated this to Beric, he set off, alone. It was mid afternoon.

Ingwar said that Sigeric would be safe for as long as Beric remembered which side he was on. He obviously didn't trust Beric or anyone else. He told the steward to make sure Sigeric and Topher didn't escape. They were serfs now and must do as they were bid. A man with arms blue to the elbow told Sigeric to follow him outside. The steward told Topher to wait by the door. Waiting, wondering what his chances of escape were, Topher heard Ingwar say he wanted to take a tour of the camp. Turning, he saw four guards heave him onto their shoulders. As they ducked to get through the doorway, he caught a glimpse of a wicker frame beneath Ingwar's scarlet cloak. Then a kick from the steward sent him flying. 'I told you not to look. Now get cleaning that.'

Serfs – it took three of them to carry it – dumped Ingwar's chain mail in front of him.

Scouring it with sand was a filthy job, but at least, sitting outside, he could see what was going on. At the other end of the thoroughfare, Sigeric had a worse job. He was stirring boiled cattle hides for the thick blue glue Vikings used to paint their shields. The reek was disgusting and if Sigeric stopped for a moment, someone yelled at him to keep stirring. Already his arms were blue. There were more Vikings in the village than he'd first thought, Topher soon realised. More and more of them kept emerging from buildings, where they'd been sleeping after travelling all night. Now they were raring for a fight. Soon whetstones screeched as they sat outside houses, sharpening swords and axes. From time to time a fight broke out. Or maybe they were just practising. The fights looked real enough, but Topher couldn't be sure.

Behind him in the hall serfs were hauling furniture about, getting ready for a feast that night. Before or after the attack? Topher wondered. Ingwar felt the cold, he learned, especially at night, so the table was being moved closer to the fire. So was his huge bed. Seeing it piled high with wolfskins, Topher thought about his grandmother and the message she'd given him. Had Ka taken it to the Abbess? What good would it do if she had? What did it say? Was the King there? If the message warned him of a Viking attack, had he got fighting men with him, enough to defend the abbey? What would they do when Beric arrived? Would they let him return?

Cooking smells and the clash of pans were coming from the next building. Soon the smell of roast meat almost masked the reek of cattle hides. When Beric hadn't returned by dusk, and serfs carried a hog on a spit into the hall, Topher's hopes rose. What if Beric didn't return? What if he'd been delayed? Perhaps the Vikings wouldn't attack after all – not tonight anyway. As warriors began to fill the hall, and the feast began, Ingwar ordered Topher to keep their beakers full to the brim. It was a chief's job to keep his men well fed and happy. Topher lost count of the number of trips he made to the vat of ale by the door. He didn't mind how many times he went, for he had a plan – to get the Danes so drunk they fell asleep. Then he'd escape to Ely, warn the nuns, and the King if he was there, about the danger facing them.

But as the night progressed, he feared he'd fall asleep before they did. The Vikings grew more warlike by the minute. They danced and stamped their feet and one or other of them kept rushing out to see if Beric was on his way back. When he hadn't returned by dark, tempers grew shorter. Ingwar, anxious to keep them happy, said, 'Get the scop. Let's have a story.'

But when a jarl with tattooed arms cut the rope holding him to the beam, the scop dropped to the floor.

'See.' Ingwar caught hold of Topher's arm. 'That's what happens if you tell stories about the Danes.'

And everyone laughed for they all took their cue from Ingwar. When he laughed they laughed. When he belched they belched. All without looking at him. And when he slumped in silence they were silent. Was the poor scop dead or alive, Topher wondered? When no one seemed to be looking, he managed to drop some bread near him, and dribble some ale on his lips. Then Ingwar made a rousing speech, saying how he would reward them with rings and heap honours on their heads when they had proved themselves in battle – and the men were on their feet again.

But at last the drink did its work, on Ingwar anyway. Yawning, he fell forward. The hammer of Thor round his neck fell into a dish of stewed leeks and he was about to follow. Two guards grabbed him just in time and the steward ordered people to leave. As jarls, warriors and serfs trailed from the hall, Topher went to join them, to escape if he could, but the steward had other ideas.

'Not you.' He grabbed his hair. 'You sleep by your lord in case he needs anything in the night. There.' He pointed to the huge bed on the other side of the fire. 'At the foot, on the floor.'

Relieved he wasn't expected to sleep with Ingwar, Topher crouched at the end of the bed and watched as four jarls lowered the huge Viking onto it. No one seemed to be watching him – the steward had gone – so he watched them unbuckling the straps that held the wicker frame together. Then lift off the front part and ease the back part from under the massive body.

'Aaaah.' Ingwar grunted as he sank into the goose down quilt.

Two guards pulled off his boots, with eyes turned away. Another removed the gold collar from round his neck. The fourth dropped a wolfskin over his lower half, but not before Topher caught a glimpse of his floppy white legs.

'Don't' – the steward returned and clouted him – 'ever let him know you saw them. Now lie down.' He pointed to the bare earth floor. 'If he wakes do exactly what he says. If you need help get the guards. They'll be by the door all night and will keep the fire stoked.'

Then he left again after snuffing out the rush light on the wall.

Escape, Topher told himself, positioning himself so he could see the guards. One had a tattoo of a dragon on his arm, the other a serpent winding right round it. He could see them clearly in the moonlight that shone through the door. *Escape*, he told himself, as Ingwar started snoring. Surely now the guards would sit down? *Escape*. But the guards stayed on their feet, spears and axes gleaming. Every now and then one of them checked the fire and piled on another log. *Escape*. But Topher felt his eyelids grow heavier. He tried to keep them open but he hadn't slept for ages. Then Serpent Arms sat down and Dragon Arms told him to have a kip. 'I'll have one later. We'll take turns.'

Serpent Arms was soon snoring and Topher's hopes rose. If only they'd both go to sleep ... and he could stay awake ...

Then he was awake, wide awake and knew he'd fallen asleep. For something had woken him. Someone. Crying. For a moment he was back at the homestead woken by one of his sisters. 'Don't! Don't! Please don't.'

No. Not his sister. Not a girl's voice. Must be a neighbour's boy.

He tried to shut out the sound, but couldn't.

'Don't! Please don't!'

Opening his eyes he remembered where he was. Kneeling up, he found himself looking at Ingwar's mountainous body.

'Don't! Please don't!' Ingwar was crying.

'Down!' Someone pushed Topher to the floor.

It was one of the guards, on his hands and knees. 'And never let him know you've seen him like this. He's having a nightmare, of when he was a little boy and his mother tried to drown him.' He seemed to forget that Topher was a Saxon who didn't understand Danish. 'His father saved him, but he can't forget his mother's curse. Now, lie down and hope he settles down.'

He – it was Dragon Arms – crawled back to his post and Topher tried to sleep, but he was wide awake now, and Ingwar was still sobbing. 'Don't, Mutti, please don't. I'll be a good boy. I'll make you proud of me. Please don't.'

It went on and on.

'Mutti. Mutti. Please don't.'

Poor thing. Topher almost felt sorry for him. But not for long. *Escape*. Could this be his chance? Pretending to be stirring in his sleep he rolled over to check the door. No. Dragon Arms was still standing in the doorway. But staring into the darkness outside he didn't see movement at his feet. Ka! She was coming in and headed straight for Topher with something in her mouth!

Eagerly he took it from her. What was it? If only the light was better. He checked the door again. The guard was still looking outside. Back to Ka, but she'd gone.

Oh no! She was on the rail at the end of the bed, and as he breathed, 'No,' she jumped onto Ingwar's legs.

'No.'

But Ka took no notice. She padded along the legs onto the mound of a body, on and on till she was standing in front of his face.

'Mutti, please don't.' Ingwar was whimpering, still pleading with his mother.

'Prrrrt.' Ka lifted her left paw and tapped the side of his face.

Topher held his breath.

'Prrrrt.' She tapped his face again – and Ingwar looked at her!

His eyes had been open all the time, but had been looking up, at the mother in his nightmare who wanted him dead. Now he was looking at Ka, whose purring was like a hive of bees.

Prrrrt. Prrrrt. They seemed to calm him. His sobs became sniffs. Then the sniffs softened. Quietened. Stopped. And she stepped forward and licked the tears from his face.

Frrrrrya. Frrrrreya.

'Freya.' Ingwar smiled. 'Freya, you come from Freya?'

Frrrrrrrrrrrr. Frrrrrrrrrrrrrrrrr.

Did Ingwar think Ka was one of the goddess's six black cats, that pulled her chariot across the heavens? She looked black in the dark.

Frrrrrrrr. Frrrrrrrrrrr.

'Really? Then why . . . ?'

126

But now Ka was rubbing her furry body against his cheeks, tickling him.

He giggled.

Rrrrrrrrrrrest. Rrrrrrrrrrest.

Still purring, she lifted one paw and then the other, pressing each of his eyelids in turn. Eyes closed now, he heaved a sigh and Ka jumped off the bed. Topher froze as he heard the guard move. But he was only moving his weight from one foot to another, still looking outside.

Ingwar began to snore. Soon his snores shook the rafters.

The guard turned to look, then sat down and closed his eyes.

Topher felt the little bundle in his hand and his heart sank. It was the one he had given Ka.

'So ... rrrry. So ... rrry.'

She hadn't delivered it. She hadn't delivered the message, whatever it had said. Somehow he'd hoped his grandmother was warning the nuns about the danger threatening them. That she was telling King Edmund about the danger facing East Engleland. But if she hadn't, he must.

Prrt. Ka ran to the door.

Both guards still seemed to be sleeping.

Topher pushed the weaving into the pouch on his belt, and crept after her. Crept past them into the darkness where there was no sign of Ka! But then he saw her green eyes shining to the left of him.

Rrrr ... un. Run.

127

Praying to the Cross God to help him, he hurried after her, for if the guards woke now he was dead.

He tried to keep running, tried to keep up with her as she zigzagged through the settlement, but the ground was uneven and he couldn't see where he was putting his feet. It was very dark and there were dead bodies lying around. Ka, though, seemed to know where she was going. She kept close to buildings. She stayed in their shadow. Sometimes he couldn't see her, but then she'd stop and turn, so he could see her eyes shining. She moved silently and he tried to, for he felt eyes watching him and ears listening. Could they get out of the settlement? Could they find the abbey? How long would it be before someone saw that he'd gone? And could they warn the nuns before the alarm went up?

Chapter 20

All was quiet in the buildings they passed, except for the rustle of straw as animals stirred, and the rumble of someone farting and snoring. But who knew what was really happening behind those wattle walls? Anyone could be spying on them. A light sleeper could easily wake at the sound of running footsteps. Ka's sight was much better than his and she seemed to be keeping away from the main track through the settlement. Where was she taking him? To the abbey he hoped. But why hadn't she gone to the abbey? Why hadn't she delivered the weaving?

She stopped. He stopped and as a ragged moon came out from behind a cloud, he saw why. He saw the abbey in front of them, but maybe a mile away. There was water in front of them. A sheet of black water. He could hear it lapping. Ely was a separate island and further away than he'd thought. But there must be a causeway over to it, like the one on the other side. So where was it? He couldn't see. A cloud covered the moon again.

Prrt. You stop here. Ka went forward to investigate.

Then her green eyes shone out of the darkness as she turned to look at him.

Prrt. Come on.

He crept towards her and found himself near a wooden hut, a gatehouse he guessed. It looked like the one on the other side. So where were the guards? There seemed to be only one and he was sleeping, sitting down with his back against the wall. And where was the causeway? It must start here. Topher strained his eyes to see in the dark but all he could see was the glassy darkness of water. Ka had disappeared again. Then he saw her eyes. Had she found the causeway?

He crept past the guard.

Yes, she'd found the causeway, but only the start of it. As the moon reappeared he saw bits of wattle and broken wood floating on the gleaming water. So that's why she hadn't gone to Ely. The Vikings had ripped up the start of the causeway.

A boat. That was Topher's first thought and there were boats, Viking longboats, moored further up. But they were much too big. He needed a small boat. Were there any skiffs near them? He went to see. The sky looked clearer, the moon brighter. A wind had got up, moving cloud across the sky, and slapping water against the bank. He looked on the bank and in the water, but couldn't see any smaller craft. And the water seemed to be getting deeper as he looked, the lapping louder, as if the tide was coming in. He was about to try and clamber up the side of a longboat to see if there was a skiff inside it, when Ka started hissing.

Sssssss. He could feel her fur bristling against his leg.

Dropping to the ground, he hid under the overhanging side of the longboat.

Sssssss. She was looking at the gatehouse.

Following her gaze he saw a large dog. Then he heard footsteps. Running footsteps. The guards were coming. He heard their voices. He saw the dog sniff the ground.

'Find! Find!' said a man in Danish and the dog looked up, then down again.

It had got his scent, he was sure of it. It was heading for him. He could see its eyes, see its lolling tongue. The game was up. The dog was loping towards him, gathering speed, and was only a man's length away when it yelped. Howled. For Ka was clinging to the side of its face. The dog was shaking its head from side to side. Ka clung on. Then she let go, dropped to the ground, took another swipe at the dog's face and ran. Yelping, it ran after her, straight back into the settlement. And Topher dropped into the water as the guards came round the side of the hut.

One saw the dog and ran after it.

The other shook the gatehouse keeper. 'Wake up, you drunken sot. Have you seen a boy go by?'

Topher, clinging to the bank, hoped they wouldn't look in his direction.

'Only just nodded off,' the keeper lied. 'Seen nobody.'

'Well, get up and help me look!'

Now they both came towards the longboats, crouching to see beneath them.

Gulping as much air as he could, Topher loosened his fingers and lowered himself beneath the water. He felt his feet touch the muddy bottom. But how long could he stay under? How long could he hold his breath? He could see the guard above him as a bubble of air escaped from the corner of his mouth. He watched it rise to the surface. Another bubble. He felt as if his chest was bursting. It was no good. He was going to have to take another breath. Felt himself rising. But as he broke the surface to a cry of 'There!' and waited for hands to grab him, no hands grabbed.

Looking out he saw the guard running away – after the dog!

Ka had got them on the run. She must have.

Thanks, Ka.

He clambered out. What now? Oh no! The gatekeeper was standing near the water's edge, looking in his direction.

'Stop, boy!' He ran forward.

And Topher ran straight at him like a ram, butting him towards the water, only just stopping himself from falling in after him. He watched the man flailing as he fell. Splash! Thud! It sounded as if he'd hit something hard. And he stopped flailing and lay still. His head must have hit one of the tree-trunk posts that had supported the causeway. This gave Topher an idea. If the posts were just under the water, perhaps he could walk on them across to the abbey? But then he heard voices. The guards were back. Silent as an otter he slid into the water again and swam, keeping under till he came to one of the posts supporting the causeway. Then clinging to it, he surfaced, just. Peering out to the shore he saw people and dogs everywhere, running and shouting, some holding flaming torches. Then someone was pointing and shouting, 'Look in the water!'

Was the game up? Feeling eyes on him, he went under again.

But when he came up, he saw that they had seen the gatekeeper's body.

Now, praying no one could see him, he turned towards the abbey. In the distance he could see lights. Ducking under water he began to swim, staying under water for as long as he could. When he did surface he could still hear shouts, so he dived underwater again. He stayed under for as long as his breath would hold. Surfaced. Heard voices. Went under again. He didn't know how many times he did this, but at last when he resurfaced all was quiet. He had left Swindune behind, but the tide was coming in. He could feel it pushing him southwards and the lights of the abbey seemed further away. Striking out westwards with as much strength as he could, he wondered how far away it was. Could he swim that far? He had never swum so far before and hoped he could keep going. Hoped no one was following. If the Vikings jumped in one of their longboats or even a skiff they could catch him easily. Treading water for a moment, he turned and looked back and saw something moving through the water.

Chapter 21

Whatever it was didn't catch him. Perhaps it wasn't chasing him. Perhaps it was a seal come up from the Wash. There were lots there he'd heard. At last he reached the other side and dragged himself onto the bank – where rough hands pulled him up by his dripping hair.

'What do you think you're doing, squit?' The tongue was Saxon, the voice deep. He thought a man had hold of him, till he saw the white wimple. 'On your knees and thank the Lord you didn't get this between your ribs.' An old nun in a grey habit brandished a spear.

'I've – c-come – to – warn – you.' It was hard speaking with his head wrenched back.

'What about?'

'Vikings.'

'Vikings!' She tightened her grip. 'Where?'

'L-let – go – I'll – t-tell – you.' His teeth were chattering now, with fear and cold. His wet cyrtle clung to his skin.

Another white wimple stepped out of the shadows. 'What is it, Sister Witberga?'

This one held a knife.

'A squit of a boy, Sister Ethelfreda. He says the Vikings are coming.'

'Well, let him speak.'

Sister Witberga loosened her grip on his arm, but kept

hold of his hair, while he delivered his warning.

'The Vikings are *here,*' he whispered for fear that his voice could carry over the water. 'Close. In the settlement called Swindune, and I have a message for the Abbess.'

They took him straight to the Abbess. Her cell was a small room furnished with a bed and table. On the table stood a lantern, six candles in a wooden frame, with panels made of see-through horn. She stood by it and it lit up her face. Old and wrinkled, like Sister Witberga, she wasn't as hairy as the fierce nun, but it was hard to tell the women apart. They all wore grey habits and white wimples. Listening intently while he told her all he knew, the Abbess noticed him start when the lantern rattled.

'Three of the clock,' she said. 'My clock, a present from Prince Alfred of Wessex. I will show you later, but first you need dry clothes.'

Looking down, he suddenly remembered his grandmother's message. Where was it?

'Why are you flapping like a fish out of water?' said the hairy nun.

'Because ...'

He was still trying to find his pouch in the wet folds of his cyrtle. It had been hanging from his belt. Where was his belt? He couldn't find it! It had gone! Belt, pouch, weaving, all had gone! When, *where* had he lost it?

'I had a message for you, the Abbess, woven into a piece of linen.'

'From whom?' said the Abbess.

'My grandmother. She said she knew you.'

135

'What is her name?'

It took him a moment to remember. 'Th-Thora.'

'Thora? Is that Thora of Haegellisdom?'

'Yes.'

'Well then,' the Abbess smiled. 'We must discuss this matter further, when you are dry. What did the message say? Do you know?'

'No.' He shook his head, wishing he could read. 'But you must send for help. Get the fyrd. The Vikings are going to attack as soon as reinforcements come!'

Act, he wanted to yell, *do* something, but the younger nun had him by the arm.

But the Abbess had acted, he learned as soon as he returned to her cell. Feeling stupid dressed in a nun's habit – tucked into a girdle to make it shorter, but still far too long – he heard a man's voice. Was it the King? That would be wonderful, but when Sister Ethelfreda opened the door, a bleary-eyed Beric stood before the Abbess.

'So whom do I believe?' she was saying. 'You who say there is no danger, or Topher who says the enemy is at the gate?'

'Do you believe a Christian man or a boy from a pagan family, Holy Mother?' Beric was bent double, trying to look humble.

'Topher's grandmother was as good a Christian as any I know,' said the Abbess.

'But sadly, the boy is a thief and liar,' said Beric. 'He fled the village and I was sent to bring him back.'

'Boys do lie,' said Sister Witberga.

136

'But why did you not say before that you had been sent to find him?' said the Abbess.

'And why would he say there was going to be a Viking attack if there wasn't?' said Sister Ethelfreda.

'To cause trouble,' said Beric. 'I assure you there are no Vikings in Swindune.'

The nuns looked at each other as if they didn't know whom to believe.

'We could put them to the ordeal,' said Sister Witberga.

'There is a better way,' said the Abbess. 'But thank you, Sister Witberga. I put you in charge of Beric. Do not let him leave. It is for your own good,' she said as Beric protested. 'Sister Ethelfreda, carry the candle clock and lead us to the church. You, Topher, stay close to me.'

'What if the boy is lying?' The fierce nun seemed to trust no one. 'Shouldn't we restrain him?'

'We shall find out soon enough,' said the Abbess. 'And he cannot run away dressed like that.'

Sister Ethelfreda picked up the clock and led the way, but Sister Witberga took off her girdle, made a loop and put it round Beric's neck. He remonstrated loudly, but the Abbess seemed not to notice as he was led from the room like a dog.

They had to cross a courtyard to reach the wooden church, the biggest church Topher had ever seen. There were other buildings all round the square, but they were all in darkness. Small windows high up the walls lit the church. When they reached the door the Abbess opened it with one of the keys hanging from her girdle, and they followed her inside. On their right was an aisle leading to an altar with a large gold cross. Candles burned on either side of it, and more candles bordered the aisle. Two nuns were kneeling at the foot of steps leading to the altar. The Abbess turned towards it and made the sign of the cross. Topher thought she was going to join the other nuns, and lead them all in prayer, but she got another key and opened a small door, just in front of them.

Beyond it was a staircase. It led to the top of the tower, the Abbess said. Now they had to go single file. Sister Ethelfreda still led the way. The Abbess followed and Topher, hitching up the long habit, followed her, trying not to trip. Beric was just behind him. Topher could feel his breath, and was glad the fierce nun had a rope round his neck. But he could hear her wheezing – she was an old woman – and he was aware that Beric's hands were free and very near his own neck. What were the chances for three nuns and a boy, if Beric decided to resist? Why had Beric stayed the night, anyway, he wondered? Because he hadn't found out if the King was there or not? He thought of the Vikings in Swindune. What if Beric didn't return? How long would it be before they came to see for themselves?

The stairs spiralled upwards and it took a while to reach the top, but at last they did. The Abbess opened another door and Sister Ethelfreda led them into a small square room. There were windows on every wall and the Abbess walked to one of them. 'This overlooks the water to Swindune. We may be able to see what is happening there.'

They all peered out, but there was nothing to see, even though there was no horn in the window. It was too dark, or perhaps Swindune was too far away. Topher didn't know what to think. It was good there were no lights moving about in the village – or on the water. That meant the search had been called off, perhaps. Someone could be rowing over in the dark. In fact, scores of Vikings could be coming over by boat. The nuns ought to be sending for help, while they could. Straining his ears to hear more clearly, he heard a sound that could be Viking oars or the wind.

'It's not long till first light,' said the Abbess. 'We shall see better then. Meanwhile we shall pray. Boy, lie down and rest.'

She had seen that Topher was finding it hard to keep his eyes open. For two nights at least he had hardly slept. So he lay down on the wooden floor, his head near the candle clock. Soon he heard a nail marking a division in the candle; it clinked as it fell into a metal tray, but nothing more.

When voices woke him it was lighter. What had the nuns seen? Nothing much it seemed, though they were looking out of the east-facing window.

Beric was saying, 'Sadly, you cannot see what is happening in Swindune, Holy Mother. It is too far and the sun is in your eyes. But I assure you again, all is well. As I said the boy likes to tell stories. He does not know where a story ends and the truth begins. I beg you, let me take him back to his parents. I am sure you need the room. Did I hear you say the guest wing was full? Who are your other guests by the way?'

There he was, still trying to find out about the King.

The Abbess didn't answer, Topher noticed, and now Sister Ethelfreda was tugging the sleeve of her habit.

'Holy Mother, l-look out of the north window.' Her voice trembled.

Topher pulled himself to his feet, but now the nuns and Beric blocked the window. It took time to wriggle between them, and stand on tiptoe. Even then, all he could see at first was the sky above and the river below, winding through the marshes. Sea birds flew over it and waders, black and white, filled the foreground. In the water, further off, were more birds, brightly coloured. Red and white. But there were no red and white birds!

'Vikings!'

He wasn't sure who screamed or what happened next. Suddenly though, Beric's face hit the floor and Sister Witberga had her foot on his back. She held the point of her spear against his neck. 'Liar! The boy tells the truth! Move and you'll be spit roast!'

The other nuns seemed frozen. Only their lips moved.

'Dear God, save us from the fury of the Northmen.

We are but poor defenceless women...'

Sister Witberga's spear still hovered over the traitor's neck. Topher saw it out of the corner of his eye. But his attention was riveted on the river. Red and white sails were getting closer. The reinforcements were on their way. A fleet of longboats was slicing through the water.

Chapter 22

Topher shook the Abbess's arm. 'Do something!'

'You are right,' said the Abbess, suddenly decisive. 'Sister, get the King from his bed.'

'There is no need,' said a rich voice from the doorway, and Topher turned to see a man dressed for action. 'In the monastery we have lookouts too.'

'Your Highness.' The sisters dropped to their knees, and so did Topher. Was this the King, the man his father thought too holy to fight? As he stayed low, Topher wished Topheric could see him. He seemed to fill the room. Though he did not wear a crown – a plain leather band held back his golden hair – he looked every inch a king. Hanging from his belt, beneath a purple cloak, was the most magnificent sword Topher had ever seen.

'Holy Mother, Sisters, rise. Stand up, boy. You are right. We must act. The fyrd must be called, but it is too late, alas, to reach the men of East Engleland. The east is cut off. I shall send riders straightway, to Wessex and Mercia to ask for aid.' He called to a retainer standing on the stairs. 'You see to that.' And to another he said, 'Tell all my men and the monks to prepare for battle, for we are going to need every man we've got.'

Then he turned to Beric, still on the floor. 'Thank you, Sister Witberga, you have done well, but my men will deal with him now.'

Two more retainers yanked Beric to his feet.

'Tell us everything you know,' said the King.

'My Lord, we haven't got much time,' said the Abbess. 'Three longboats approach.'

'So, seventy or eighty men are coming this way,' said the King. 'And we have but fifty here.'

Fifty! Where were they? Topher wondered.

The King turned back to Beric. 'What do you know of their plans?'

'N-n-n-n-nothing,' the basket maker gibbered.

'He lies,' said Topher. 'There are at least another fifty men over the water in Swindune, with their leader, Ingwar the Boneless.'

'So they outnumber us more than two to one,' said the King. 'Even with the monks, but some of them were once doughty fighters.'

'And they will fight again,' said the Abbess. 'Please, take that scoundrel away.'

As Beric was dragged from the room Topher told the King all he knew.

'Ingwar has been waiting for his brothers. All three are intent on avenging their father's death and conquering our island. But' – he remembered something else – 'he is waiting for Beric to tell him if you are here in Ely.'

The King nodded. 'He'll wait a long time, then.'

'We must pray for them to wait,' said the Abbess, 'for we desperately need time.'

'Two days at least,' said the King. 'For Wessex and Mercia are at least a day's ride away.'

Sister Ethelfreda and Sister Witberga were already on their knees.

'Dear God, save us from the fury of the Northmen. We are but poor women . . .'

As the nuns prayed, the King sent orders that every man on the island – his thanes and all the monks – was to surround the abbey in case of attack. 'But well hidden,' he said. 'For if they see fighting men they may guess I am here. If it looks undefended they might think I am not and delay their attack.' Then he dropped to his knees and joined the nuns in prayer.

And Topher thought about the Vikings across the water, eager for action. Wouldn't they suspect that the King was there when Beric didn't return? Somehow he couldn't see Ingwar waiting long, not now he had reinforcements.

He touched the King's robe. 'Your Highness!'

A retainer hauled him back. 'A carl does not address a king!'

But the King stood up. 'I would hear the boy.'

Topher dropped to his knees. 'Your Highness, I do not think the Vikings will wait long, and I have another idea.' Humbly, he did not say a better idea. 'Would it not be better to make it look as if we have *more* than fifty men? Many more. Could not the nuns as well as the monks dress as warriors? Could we not all arm ourselves or look as if we are armed? It is a trick I learned from the Vikings,' he added as the King raised an eyebrow.

Down below in the courtyard there was clatter of hoofs.

143

'God speed,' said the King. 'My riders are on their way to Wessex and Mercia.'

'God speed,' said the Abbess, moving to the King's side to look out of the west window.

Then they all moved back to the north window, and Topher thought for a moment the nuns' prayers had been answered, for there was no sign of the longboats. No red and white sails at all. Had they turned back? Had they all sunk? Had there been a marvellous miracle! He watched the water for signs of sinking ships and floundering bodies, but instead saw something glinting. There was a flash of gold and then another. The boats were still approaching, with lowered sails. Their gilded prows gleamed in the light of the rising sun.

The nuns started praying.

'Lord of the rushing waves, save us.
Forgive us our sins ...'

Making the sign of the cross, Topher joined in.

'Lord of the flowing wind, save us.
Forgive us our sins ...'

But when he opened his eyes the boats were closer still. He could see rowers propelling the boats through the water. Getting closer and closer. The prow of the first one was a gilded dragon's head. There was a wolf's head on the mainmast. The wolf was Bjorn's emblem, so the man at the helm with long grey hair blown forward by the wind was Ingwar's brother. He looked a bit like a wolf, but his forearms, gleaming with silver, showed he

144

was a warrior of many battles. Behind him sat a score of oarsmen, and now he turned to them.

Go on to Thetford. Go on to Thetford. Topher willed them to sail past Ely and Swindune, but they didn't. They laid down their oars. Bjorn's shouts were orders to stop. Now they leaned back, oars dangling, and Topher saw the fighting men filling the longboat. Archers with bows on their backs stood up and stretched. Swordsmen flexed their muscles, and stacked in the bows were helmets, spears, long-shafted war axes and shields. Topher's heart sank when he saw the shields, a sure sign the Danes were intent on war. So was the dragon on the prow, for when Danes came trading the shields decorated the sides of the ship, and the dragon was stowed in the bilge. But when Vikings came raiding the dragon was to the fore to frighten the land spirits of the land they were about to attack.

The boats behind them were slowing down too. Was that Hvitserk at the helm of the second longboat? The prow was a gilded serpent. A bristling boar's head topped the mainmast. His oarsmen laid down their oars. What was happening? For a while they seemed still. Then Bjorn shouted something, the other helmsmen repeated what he'd said, and half the rowers picked up their oars and the boats turned towards Ely. So they weren't sailing on to Thetford. They were mooring at Swindune. Topher imagined the whoops of joy when Ingwar's men saw them.

He hadn't noticed the others joining him at the window, for all four, the nuns and the King, were silent, struck dumb by the imminent danger. Then he felt a hand on his shoulder and turned to see the King looking at him, as a nun ran in with more news. A stranger had arrived at the west gate in the night, she said.

'He comes from Swindune and he asks for you, Your Highness. He is in the church.'

The man was slumped on the ground, his back against the white marble tomb of Saint Etheldreda, the church's founder. Two of King Edmund's men guarded him, though he looked too frail to resist. At first Topher did not recognise him, for his head was in his hands, but when he looked up he saw it was the scop. Thinner than when he had last seen him, there was a red blister on his face where the guard had held the flaming torch. One arm hung limply by his side and a crutch lay on the floor beside him.

'You're alive.' Topher was amazed.

'Just,' the man nodded. 'Thanks to you.'

The King was wary. 'How did you know Topher was here?'

'I didn't. The Danes think he drowned. I hoped and I trusted the cat.'

Cat! It was only then that Topher noticed Ka, though she was rubbing round his legs, throbbing with purrs. He bent down to stroke her, as the King asked the scop more questions.

'How did you get out of Swindune?'

The scop gasped as if it hurt him to speak. 'The Danes – gave me up for dead – threw me on a heap – I waited till dark – then crawled to the edge of the island – hid in

146

water – till the cat found me – wondrous animal – led me to skiff – first we went south – then doubled back to warn – you.'

'What of?' said the King.

'That – there – is – no – hope,' gasped the scop. 'I tried – to – reach – you – sooner – but – that – scoundrel – Beric – got – word – to – the – Danes – and – they – took – me – prisoner.'

It was some moments before he could speak again. 'No hope at all. The Danish forces are massive. Bjorn and Hvitserk have come by river. Sigurd has come overland and Guthrum is on the east coast with a fleet. He has brought five hundred men across the North Sea.'

'Five hundred!' Sister Ethelfreda's mouth fell open.

'Five – hundred – eager – for battle. At – the – mouths – of – rivers – north – south – and east. More – wait – Thetford. East – Engleland – is – surrounded.'

'So when will they attack? How long have we got?'

'No time,' said the scop. 'Ingwar – has read – the signs. Ravens – circling – overhead. Woden – saying – time – right. Warriors – straining – at – leash – like – hunting – dogs. May – wait – morrow, Thorsday – may not.' He closed his eyes, exhausted.

Prrt. Prrt. Ka padded up to him and patted his face.

He opened his eyes. 'Ah yes. This.' He fumbled with his belt, Topher's belt! It was slimy as if it had been in water, but with the pouch still attached! Topher knelt and loosened the drawstring. He pulled out the weaving and spread it on the ground. The wet made the runes stand out clearly. He saw his name. His grandmother had taught him to read that. But what did the other words say?

ᚺᚪ ᚠᛋ ᛏᚪᚳᚻᛗᚱ ᛒᛁᚾᛋ

The Abbess read them aloud. 'Do as Topher bids.'

Everyone turned to look at Topher, then at the scop, who, looking straight at him, was speaking in a halting whisper.

'There – will – come – a hero – with a – torn hem.

He'll – help – but won't – stop – these – very – bad . . .'

'Men.' Topher finished for him, and felt a hand on his shoulder.

He looked up into the King's blue eyes.

'Topher, what does he mean?'

'He means me,' said Topher, who could hardly believe it himself. 'My cyrtle – it's drying – it has a torn hem.'

'He is right,' said Sister Ethelfreda. 'I saw it myself.'

'Then we must do as you say,' said the Abbess.

'With all haste,' said King Edmund.

Chapter 23

Do as Topher bids.

The King acted as if it was a command from God, not Topher's grandmother. For the rest of the day he kept Topher by his side as he strode round the abbey, checking that everyone was carrying out his orders. Topher prayed that if it came to a fight he would have good courage, for it was in battle that a boy became a man. He hoped though to deter the Vikings with a show of force and huge numbers.

In the refectory they found nuns worked swiftly with shears and needles and thread to turn habits into hose and britches and cyrtles. Outside in the courtyard, others were whittling broom handles and branches into spears. Others, taking a lead from Sister Witberga, had whipped off their wimples and were now spiking their short hair with candle wax. Now they looked like the Celtic warriors Topher had heard stories about. Seeing them, the Vikings might well think the Saxons had got help from the tribes in the west.

Later they came across Sister Witberga again. This time she was drilling her troops in the courtyard. In men's clothes they looked fearsome, and the King told her to take them to the side of the island facing Swindune, where his men had already taken up positions. From afar it would look as if Ely was well defended – if the Vikings didn't go round the other side where defenders were sparser. Topher wondered what they could do about that and thought of another ruse.

Soon there were heads at every window, heads made of bundles of cloth wearing helmets made of cooking pots. And poking out of the windows were long bows made of branches. On the shore there were more broomsticks stuck in the ground, with cabbage heads and cloth bodies. The King sounded full of faith as he walked round the abbey, encouraging everyone. He said he was sure they could hold out till reinforcements arrived from Wessex and Mercia. But the scop, when they went back to him in the church, had neither faith nor hope. Still slumped on the ground, his face was the same colour as the white marble tomb behind him.

'My Lord,' he gasped, 'the fyrd from Mercia will not come. The Mercians blame you for giving horses and winter shelter to the Vikings, for they used the horses to take Snotengahan and Hreathandune.'

It did not do for a commoner to gainsay a king, and Topher thought the King might be angry. But he shook his head and then walked down the aisle, to lie face down before the gold altar. They heard him ask God for forgiveness. Then the door opened and the Abbess, in britches and cloak, seemed to fly down the aisle and nearly tripped over him.

'Forgive me, Your Highness. I did not see you there, but we must bury the holy cross now.' Two of the King's men were with her. Again, Topher thought he might

150

protest, but he got to his feet and told his men to do the Abbess's bidding.

Now Topher noticed that the church was nearly bare. The nuns had been busy. There were no tapestry pictures on the walls, no golden chalice or silver plate on the altar. The candlesticks lining the aisle had gone. Did this mean that the Abbess thought the Vikings would come? *He'll help but won't stop these very bad men.* The words in his head were not encouraging. And now four nuns rushed in, still in their habits and wimples. Seeming not to see the poor scop, they each went to a corner and tried to lift the marble tomb. When they couldn't they started wailing.

'Sisters!' The Abbess flew back down the aisle. 'What can't be helped must not be wept over. Go and do something useful! Garb yourself as men. Get arms! Go! Shoo!'

But before they could, the door to the tower opened, and a man rushed out shouting.

'VIKINGS! THE VIKINGS ARE COMING!'

'They have set off from Swindune. They are coming this way!'

The King swept past to see for himself, and Topher followed him to the top of the tower. From the east window they saw the boats.

'I must go and face them,' said the King, hand on sword. 'I must lead my men.'

'No, Your Highness, not yet.' For, as Ka came into the room, Topher had another idea. 'Your Highness, I think you should stay hidden.'

'Like a cowering dog?' The King shook his head.

'No, like a waiting lion,' Topher replied. 'If we have to fight you will lead us, but if we can delay the battle . . .'

'That would be good,' agreed the King.

'Well, as you said, if they see you they will attack straightway. If they don't they might wait, or they might come ashore and search for you. Whatever, it will give us time, and we need time. So, please, Your Highness, let me – and Ka – do what we can.'

King Edmund put his hand on Topher's head. 'Bless you and God speed. I shall be watching and I shall be by your side if battle begins.'

Topher hurried downstairs, Ka close to his heels. He didn't know exactly what he was going to do, but he hoped and prayed he – they – could do something to stop the Viking leader. Ravens circled overhead. Woden's birds, and it was Woden's day. Their glossy black shapes made patterns against the blue dome of sky, now streaked gold in the west. Ingwar would think the birds a good omen, but surely tomorrow, Thor's day, would be better for war? If only he could make him think that. From time to time a bird wheeled so low he could see its wings with feathers outstretched like fingers.

'God's birds,' said the Abbess, suddenly by his side. He hadn't noticed her leave the church. 'They are all God's birds.'

They crossed the courtyard together and walked between two buildings, which brought them into the

152

open. Now they could see the sea and the boats, closer now. Ka turned left and ran towards the causeway.

'Stay here, Holy Mother.' But as Topher tried to follow the Abbess took hold of his arm. 'It's too dangerous. You will be a target for their bowmen.'

He said, 'Please, remember my grandmother. Do as she bid.'

Reluctantly she let him go.

Ka was standing on the causeway now, looking at something. Following her gaze, he saw something too. There were people on the causeway, so it must have been mended.

'Who are they, Ka?' He could feel her fur against his legs.

Ingwa...rrrrrr.

'You're right, of course.' He hadn't needed to ask. One man, very tall, was on horseback.

Ingwa...rrrrrrr. Ingwa...rrrrrrrr. Was Ka purring or growling? He remembered their last encounter.

There were, he thought, four men with the Viking leader, and many more beside them, in the water. Five longboats were heading for Ely, three on the north side of the causeway, two on the south. At least a hundred and fifty Viking warriors were heading for the abbey, where ninety Saxon men and women were waiting to defend it. Could the Danes see him? Topher wondered. Could they see Ka? He thought they must be able to see him, though the setting sun was in their eyes. The causeway shuddered beneath his feet as they got nearer.

The wattle hurdles creaked. Soon he could hear harsh Danish voices, and one squeaky one.

'Who is that?'

'A boy, my Lord,' answered one of the guards. 'I think it's the one who escaped.'

'So why does he stand waiting for us?'

'The gods are delivering him to our laps, Lord.'

The Vikings got closer and closer and the causeway creaked and trembled. Or was he trembling? Topher tried to stand firm, though a small voice in his head said, 'Run while you've got the chance.' Then, when it was about thirty paces away, Ingwar's horse stopped, suddenly, and Ingwar urged it forward angrily. But the animal wouldn't move. Its ears lay back and it tried to go backwards as the four guards held onto it. Topher could see the whites of its rolling eyes as a guard said, 'It's the cat, Lord. The horse is afraid of the cat.'

Now Topher saw Ka out in front, standing in the middle of the causeway – and so did Ingwar. But would he remember her? After all, when he'd seen her last, he'd been asleep, having a nightmare. He seemed to be saying something to his guards. He *was* saying something insistently. What? At last Topher made sense of his high-pitched commands.

'Lift me *down*!'

It took them several minutes to lift him off and while they did Ka watched intently, her tail upright like a quivering flame.

'What now, Lord?' For a few moments the gasping

guards held the frame high, and Ingwar's long legs, encased in boots and hose, dangled in the air. Then the horse, freed of all restraint, backed away.

'Down. There.' Ingwar pointed to the surface of the causeway and they lowered him onto it, so he was facing Ka – and Topher – with his legs splayed out in front of him.

'Stand back,' he squeaked, 'but stay close.'

When the guards were about six paces behind him, Ingwar put out his right hand and wiggled his fingers. 'Puss.'

Topher held his breath and everything went still. It was as if the whole earth held its breath. The wind stopped blowing. The longboats stopped moving through the water and on the causeway Ka was like a statue except for her quivering tail.

'Puss.' Again Ingwar wiggled his fingers. 'Where have you come from?'

Frrrrrrrr ... eya. Frrrrrrrrrr ... eya. Now Ka began to purr. Topher had never heard her purr so loudly.

'From Freya?'

Frrrrrrrrrrrrr ... eya. Frrrrrrrrrr ... eya. Purring like a swarm of bees on a summer day, Ka lowered herself onto the causeway and lay there, tail twitching, wiggling her bum. Then she pounced onto Ingwar's fingers – and he giggled. For several minutes she played with them, as if they were mice, biting one, then another. Then she jumped onto his lap and looked into his eyes intently.

Turrrrrrrrrrn back. Turrrrrrrrrrn back.

'Freya says "turn back"?'

Ka nodded. *Turrrrrrrrrrrn back. Turrrrrrrrrrrn back.*

But would he? Still the world seemed to hold its breath, and Topher, his eyes fixed on Ka, saw the Viking leader grow. He got bigger and bigger and so did the cage round his body. Suddenly his feet were as big as boulders, his legs like walls and Ka looked tiny.

'Freya says "turn back"?' His eyes bulged with amazement.

Then the ravens came.

'Ker! Ker!'

Swooping low, they circled Ingwar's head.

'Ker! Ker!' Topher could see their beaks opening and closing as they croaked. And when one of them flew down, past Ingwar's astonished face, he could see his open mouth, a red cave. But then all he could see was the same bird, coming towards him, then flying overhead, its clawed feet dangling directly above him. As he feared for his life, the hooks came lower and lower, nearer and nearer and he was too scared to move. But they rushed past, missing him by inches, as the bird landed behind him, on the wattle surface. Only then did he realise what had happened. Ingwar hadn't grown. He had shrunk!

'Ker!' Bigger than he was, it looked over its shoulder with round yellow eyes.

'Ker!' Its beak was like the tip of a sword.

'Mwow!' Suddenly Ka was by his side, her head level

with his. Then she was running up the bird's tail onto its glossy back.

'Mwow!' She turned and looked down on him. *Come on.*

First, tentatively, he felt the tail feathers with his fingers. Then, finding them firm and springy, he stepped on and clambered up, parting the feathers slightly as he gripped. But they held firm and when he reached the top, the bird lifted up its tail, sliding him down into the hollow of its back. For a moment or two he lay there rocking, then he got into a kneeling position and put his arms round the bird's neck. Ka ducked under his arm and nestled between his knees, and the bird started to walk in a circle as if it were taking bearings. Clinging on, he saw the river on either side of them wide and muddy and slow. He saw Ingwar looking down in amazement and he heard him squeak, 'Turn back!'

'Turn back?' The guards wondered if they'd heard right.

'Turn back!' Ingwar squeaked again, louder.

He saw the longboats, their gilded prows glinting in the evening sun, but before he could tell if the boats were moving or not, he felt a surge of energy under him, and he had to hold tight as the bird took off.

Up and up it went, till the river was below them, a winding brown girdle specked with red and white. Up and up and up till it was like a thread and he could see the whole of East Engleland below him, round and bulging like a big green apple – with ants crawling across it. But they weren't ants. They were long lines of

157

people, armies on the move. As the bird's wings flapped on either side of him, and the wind whipped back his hair, Topher knew he was watching help coming from the west, the Wessex fyrd that King Edmund had sent for, but also enemy forces – and there were far more of them – coming from north and south and east, by road and rivers and sea. Massive armies were gathering to do battle.

As he flew higher and higher out of danger Topher thought about the families caught between those armies. He thought about the family he had left behind in Haegellisdom. He thought about the nuns and monks, and the King and his men in Ely. Then as shapes and colours blurred and his head began to nod, he thought of nothing for he fell asleep. When he woke he knew he had passed through space and time and dimensions he couldn't name, because a familiar sight was below him. Great Britain, still amazingly green, seemed to be coming towards him at a rapid pace, but he of course was heading for it. Closer, closer, closer. There was the river Thames, a silver ribbon winding from west to east in swirling S-shapes. Here were the roofs of London coming towards him scarily fast. Lego-like buildings took seconds to become so big he thought he was going to hit them, though the bird was braking. He felt its body taut beneath him, pulling back its wings, wheeling to the left to avoid the Post Office tower, wheeling to the right to avoid the building that looked like a gherkin, getting lower, lower, lower, so he could hear sirens blaring, see blue lights flashing, smoke rising and then grass.

Chapter 24

'What are you doing with that crow, lad?' A man was standing in front of Topher, pointing between his feet, where a large black bird stood on the grass.

How had that got there? How had he got here? He moved a leg and it flapped into the air, reminding him of something, but he didn't know what.

'Topher, there you are!' A boy grabbed his arm and the man wandered off. 'Where have you been, mate? I thought for a bit ...'

Where had he been? A ragged scrap of memory surfaced, and he checked to see that he was normal-sized. He looked at the boy and then down at himself. The boy was bigger, but that was because he was sitting.

'It's me, Sanjit, mate.'

Sanjit. Sanjit? Where was he?

'Think you've got concussion, mate. Look, there's Ellie.' He pointed to a girl sitting on the grass with her head in her hands. 'You stay here, I'll go see her.'

They seemed to be in a park. There were other people nearby – a woman in a sari, a woman with a pushchair and a bare-chested man – and more people were streaming into the park through a side gate. On the other side of some railings was a big red bus.

'Oh, yes.' He started to remember what had happened

before his journey to the past. An explosion. So why was the bus still in one piece?

'Amazing.'

'What mate?' Sanjit was back, standing in front of him.

'Bus. Roof still on.' He remembered the man fumbling with his bag, with the bomb – it must have been a bomb – and then a bang, and then the man rising into the air and hitting his head on the roof. He saw it again in slow motion, the rapt expression on the man's face as he rose and as his head hit the roof, as he came down and crumpled onto the floor. He recalled the eye-stinging smell like Tally's nappy on a bad day, or bad eggs, or something in the lab at school.

'I thought he'd blown us all up.'

'Me too. There he is, look.' Sanjit pointed to a man coming through the gate, held firmly by two other men. Eyes closed, his face was spattered with blood and there was yellow sticky stuff on his jeans.

'Yeah.'

Now police officers were coming through the gate, and other people in uniform, paramedics in green.

People started talking then, or perhaps he just started hearing their voices. It was as if someone had turned up the volume.

'There was an explosion.'

'But it didn't go off, not properly.'

'It went off but . . . '

'The roof's still on!' That was the amazing thing. The only damage seemed to be some shattered windows.

'Nobody dead.'

'Thanks to these boys.'

Someone was patting him on the back. 'Thanks, lad. You're a hero.'

Really? Was that true about no one dead? He saw someone lying on the grass. Several people.

'Come on.' Sanjit pulled him to his feet and steered him to the girl with her head in her hands.

'Ellie, meet Topher. Topher, meet Ellie.'

They sat down either side of her. Ellie! Of course he remembered his friend, but was this really her? Ellie was talkative. Ellie was bossy. This girl was quiet, far too quiet, and she still had her head in her hands.

'You all right?' He put his arm round her.

She shook her head.

'You're hurt? Where? Tell us.' He couldn't bear Ellie to be hurt.

She shook her head again.

'Ellie, talk to us.'

'It's shock.' A policewoman had crouched down beside them. 'Do you need first aid? Do you feel cold?' She called over a paramedic who was handing out blankets and foil sleeping bags.

Topher tried again. 'Ellie, *please* say something.'

And she did at last take her hands away from her face.

'You guys,' she whispered. 'I'll never, *never* get over this.'

''Course you will.' Topher gave her a hug.

'We all will.' Sanjit was philosophical. 'People get over much worse things than this.'

But Ellie shook her head again and Topher clamped

his mouth shut, for the words 'Don't be so negative' were on the tip of his tongue.

The rest of the day passed slowly, as they were all longing to go home. They all rang their families to tell them they were all right, and ask to be picked up, but then they had to go to the hospital to be checked over. They also had to give statements to the police. While they waited to be collected, reporters, dozens of them, interviewed them for newspapers and TV and photographers took photos.

Topher didn't think about the past much till evening when he was reunited with Ka. She was there when he got back to Ellie's house, a real cat curled up on his bed! He threw himself on it, ecstatic to see her, and she was to see him. As she rubbed her face against his, her purrs were like a hive of bees. They made him think of his Saxon family and he wondered what had happened to them.

Later he logged into Ellie's computer to see what he could find out. Ellie, still strangely quiet, said he could. She stayed downstairs watching *News 24*, but he'd had enough of The Bomb That Didn't Go Off Properly. *News 24* had covered it from every angle, even BOY STOPS BOMB, which wasn't strictly true. He hadn't stopped it, but he may have stopped a few people getting injured. He couldn't help feeling proud, but it was embarrassing hearing himself being interviewed. People kept asking him how he'd known the man was fumbling with a bomb, and he couldn't say. Even now he couldn't explain it. He'd had a hunch, that was all, a lucky hunch.

But was it luck which saved the nuns of Ely and King Edmund when he was there? When was he there? He searched but couldn't find anything on the net about what he'd witnessed. Or about his Saxon family, or about an amazing cat who had charmed a Viking chief. There was plenty of information about Ely Abbey, which had been destroyed by the Danes in 869. There was quite a lot about Ingwar the Boneless who went on to become King of Dublin. There was a bit about the Battle of Haegellisdom, so he hadn't prevented that. In 870, King Edmund had led the Anglo-Saxons into battle, but the Danes, led by Ingwar, won. When King Edmund refused to bow down before him, Ingwar ordered his archers to tie him to a tree and use him for target practice. Edmund had died pierced by arrows, looking like a porcupine. Not content with that, Ingwar then had his head cut off. Later though, miraculously, Edmund's head rejoined his body and other miracles started to happen. So he became Saint Edmund. There is a city and a cathedral, Bury St Edmunds, named after him.

'Well, Ka, at least he became famous.'

She was still on his bed sleeping.

'Who became famous?' Sanjit came into the room, followed by Ellie, who still looked tragic. She was reading the *Evening Standard*.

'King Edmund.' Topher logged off, wishing he could cheer Ellie up.

'Never heard of him,' said Sanjit.

'You two, though,' Ellie spoke at last. 'Everybody's heard of you. You're in all the papers, and look out there.' She pointed out of the window. 'There are still reporters and photographers outside the house. You're really famous.'

'Oh, is that the problem?' said Sanjit. 'Is that why you'll *never, never, never get over* this?' He did a fair imitation of Ellie's tragic voice. 'Because – we – were – right and you were wrong. Well, I think if you humbly apolo—'

But he didn't finish because Ellie had him in an arm lock. She wouldn't let him go till he said he'd got something really, really important to say.

'What?' She loosened her grip – slightly.

'My bibi and my auntie have been cooking all day, and they sent me round to invite you all, everyone, the whole family, to come and celebrate being alive with a huge Indian feast.'

'With chapattis and parothas and samosas and that sweet honey cake I like?' asked Ellie.

'Yes,' said Sanjit. 'All of them.'

'Deal.' Ellie let go of his arm, and they all headed for the door.

GLOSSARY OF ANGLO-SAXON &
VIKING WORDS

carl – a peasant farmer, a tenant who does not own land

causeway – a raised road or path through a marsh or across water

cyrtle – a short tunic worn by men and boys

Freya – Nordic goddess of love and fertility and war

fyrd – an army of men called upon to fight when needed by the king

fowler – a man who catches wild fowl for cooking

gainsay – to deny, go against or disagree with

Haegellisdom – old name for Hellesdon, meaning Haegel's hill

Haligmonath – holy month, time of harvest festival, September

Hreathandune – Repton

jarl – a Danish noble, an earl

lyre – a small harp

Medehamstede – Peterborough

moot – a gathering, a meeting

nordic – from northern Europe

retainer – a person of high rank serving the king

runes – the letters of the Anglo Saxon alphabet

saga – a story, especially about a hero

scop – a storyteller, poet or minstrel

serf – a person owned and controlled by another, a slave

Snotengahan – Nottingham

steward – a person in charge of a noble's household

thane – a noble, holding land on condition he would fight for the king if called upon

Thor – Nordic god of thunder

tithing – a group of ten people responsible for keeping each other in order

wergild – money paid to a dead person's family by the murderer

Woden – Nordic god of wisdom and war, chief god

ABOUT THE AUTHOR

Julia Jarman lives in a north Bedfordshire village with her husband and Perdita the cat – an inspiration! She loves visiting schools and libraries to do talks about her stories. Urged to write by her three children ("Write about children like us – and put lots of scary bits in!"), she has written fourteen novels for Andersen Press, including the Time-Travelling Cat series.

She likes pigs and plays, cats and computers, food – growing, cooking and eating it – and books. For more info visit her happy, zappy, snappy website www.juliajarman.com